THE IRRESISTIBLE SPARK

APPLEBOTTOM MATCHMAKER SOCIETY

ABBY TYLER

SUMMARY

When a woman sets her ex-boyfriend's old memories on fire, the blaze draws a volunteer fireman who just might be able to rekindle the spark in both their broken hearts.

AbbyTyler
PO Box 160116
Austin, TX 78716
www.abbytyler.com

Paperback ISBN: 9781938150869

Edition 1.0

MEETING MINUTES

APPLEBOTTOM TOWN SQUARE PROPRIETORS
Gertrude Vogel, secretary
Because nobody else pays a lick of attention.

Today we met at the Applebottom Pie Shoppe, owned by yours truly.

Everybody wanted to talk about the recent wedding. Betty Johnson, owner of Tea for Two, and Delilah Jones, owner of the dog bakery, didn't even bother to ask if we had an agenda.

I tried to remind them that this was an official meeting, but Delilah plumped her crazy beehive and said we ought to change our name to the Applebottom Matchmaker Society. Everybody raised their coffee mugs like this was the greatest proclamation since Abraham Lincoln.

I butted in and reminded them that this was a

business organization, and Betty piped up again, saying her granddaughter Lorelei was a straight-up hot mess and maybe we could find a lovely gentleman for her, too.

Topher and Danny Smith-Cole, co-owners of Applebottom Blossoms, chimed in to say we had done a bang-up job of finding good fits already, and the whole lot of them started listing off the names of single men around town we could send on an errand to help Lorelei.

I banged the pie server like a gavel and said we didn't need to be meddling in any more young people's lives. They can get on SnapWit or Tender or whatever and find their own dates.

Betty's face pinked right up, and she said Lorelei had scarcely left the room she was renting at Linda's, and the only thing that might get her over the breakup is a new man.

Maude Lewis, the co-owner of Applebottom Pie Shoppe, took the pie server from me and started slicing our latest pear-apple creation. Everyone was quiet for a moment as they admired the interior of the pie.

As they should.

T-bone, our illustrious mayor and owner of the RV Park, said maybe the girl just needed a hobby. Did she even have a job?

Betty said, no, she'd been living on the last college

loan she took before she dropped out and spent her days making charm bracelets to sell online.

Danny and Topher, always the bleeding hearts, assured Betty that they would keep watch for an eligible young man coming through their floral shop. Maybe they could even accidentally send some flowers to her from one of them to spark a connection.

I told them that sounded like plot of a bad sitcom and if Lorelei wanted to waste her life pining over some man, they should all leave her to it.

The whole room got quiet, and I could tell every last one of them wanted to make some snarky remark about Alfred Felmont, who is a pillar of our community and a fine picture of a man on the side. So I started passing out plates to get their pie-holes busy before they really chapped my cowhide.

Maude told Betty that they'd figure something out, and insisted I put finding a man for Lorelei at the top of our agenda for next month, if nothing happened in the meantime.

Meeting adjourned.

CHAPTER 1

*T*his rage-inducing junk was going to *burn*.

Lorelei Spencer tossed another concert T-shirt out the second story window of her upstairs apartment. She'd never liked that band anyway. *He* had always made her go.

He-who-would-not-be-named.

She picked up a sheaf of greeting cards he'd given her over the years. Grocery store messages with nothing but a signature at the bottom, and maybe a short phrase.

Happy Birthday, Babe.

Happy Valentine's, Babe.

Oh, how she hated *Babe.*

"Good riddance to Babe," she muttered as the cards sailed out the window to land on the pile below.

She leaned out. The woman who rented her the

space would have a fit if she saw the mess. Good thing she was at a quilting bee with her friends. Lorelei liked her fine, but she was a judgmental thing. If she spotted Lorelei throwing trash on her lawn, she'd go through yet another spiel.

What a shame that an old person living on social security had to rent out her house to young people who didn't take care of anything anymore.

To that, Lorelei tossed a flutter of magazines, all subscriptions to *Gamer Z*, which she'd constantly read to keep up with all the video games he used to play. If she didn't, she wouldn't understand half the things he talked about.

"Farewell, zombies. Adieu, race cars. Goodbye, dragon quests, hitmen, and portals." The slick pages rained down onto the dying grass, brown and crispy after a long summer.

"And goodbye GARY!" There. She'd said his name.

The tossing of Gary's things was symbolic. He didn't live with her and never had. And truth be told, it had been a year since they were together.

Only on the anniversary of their split had Lorelei come out of her strange, misery-induced stupor. Here she was, twenty-four years old, and she'd wasted three years on this man. Plus a bonus year of moping!

Time to clean house.

She paused, considering a white bear Gary had given her on their first anniversary. She'd slept with it for a long time, kissing it goodnight when her boyfriend had spent his evenings elsewhere.

"Sorry, Fuzzy Wuzzy," she said. "Time to go." She tossed him out the window.

Then she chucked the lamb and the cat and the matching set of beagles. She had two identical stuffed dogs because Gary apparently forgot he'd already given her that exact stuffie the year before. That boy did not pay attention.

And what was with all the plush anyway? She'd never gotten any other kind of gift, other than the random box of chocolates.

She looked out. The collection was looking good. It made a nice little pile.

Now for the notebooks.

The journals were something Lorelei had started when she first met Gary. She kept meticulous details about everything he liked. Food. TV shows. Bands. She had an entire notebook devoted to songs they had listened to together. She'd listed which ones he liked to sing out loud in his deep slightly off-key voice, and which ones made him cringe. At the time, her own playlists were adapted specifically to his tastes.

Why had she done that?

She ripped a few pages angrily from the first notebook but realized they would flutter away in the breeze. If they littered other yards than her own, that would really get the neighbors going. They prided themselves on a tidy street.

Instead, she tossed the entire first notebook to the ground, where it landed on the pile with a thud. But that didn't feel satisfying.

Lorelei experimented and figured out that if she wadded five or six sheets together, it made a ball heavy enough to land in her pile.

She proceeded to rip out sections of pages from each notebook, creating a little game with herself. How accurately could she make a list of Gary's preferences fall? What about the names of his extended family, including his bratty younger siblings? And the type of toilet paper he liked, and which way to put it on the roll?

Her pile was becoming impressive. Had she really collected that much useless information related to Gary?

She decided not to stop there. She began gathering things that were hers, and were purchased by her, but still felt connected to her old relationship.

Like the bedspread. She'd bought it only to impress him, since she'd been using a Hello Kitty one up until then. She'd been a sophomore in college and wanted to invite him to her dorm room but not give the impression she was a baby.

So she'd gotten this grown-up looking comforter, yellow-gold and patterned with leaves.

She hated it. It had to go. Hello Kitty was still in her closet.

The giant wad of fabric resisted pushing through the window, but she got it done. It landed on the pile with a satisfying plop.

What about that outfit she'd bought for their first date? She never wore it anymore. For one, it was out of style. Probably it didn't even fit anymore either.

And every time she saw it, she thought of Gary.

That was reason enough.

She tossed the charcoal mini skirt out the window. It fluttered briefly before landing on the pile. Then the red cotton tank top. And the white off-the-shoulder shirt Gary had told her was the thing that originally caught his eye.

Lorelei leaned out the window to admire her pile. Now what was she going to do with it? She'd just made a mess she'd have to clean up.

Like the whole relationship.

She turned back to her room. Three free-standing candles sat on a glass plate.

The glass plate was hers, given to her by her mother, but the candles she had gotten to create a romantic ambience for one dinner or another with Gary.

Those needed to go.

She picked up all three of them, as well as a little book of matches from a restaurant in Fayetteville they had visited early on. Back when he still was interested in nights out, instead of spending all his nights *in*.

Lorelei took the three candles and the matches and headed down the stairs.

She knew exactly what she was going to do with that pile.

&

Micah Livingston leaned back in his chair in his small law office just off of Applebottom's Town Square. His desk was covered with printouts, receipts, and lines circled angrily in red by his client.

He would have to travel to St. Louis tomorrow to deal with this case. It was a thorny estate probate. The man had died after a long separation from his wife, but the pair had never divorced.

All the heirs were contentious. The man had children by three other women, two of them former wives. But the final wife had no children by him.

What a mess. One child outside of marriage with only a birth certificate to prove paternity. Four children in two divorces. And this late-in-life marriage that hadn't worked out. The actual wife was a kindly lady who wasn't trying to get involved, but unfortunately their legal status with no prenup meant she had to be.

He sighed. He often saw the ugliness that wrecked a family over money.

His secretary, Marianne, buzzed through on the intercom. "Micah, you've got a fire call."

Great. Just what he needed the day before a huge case. To go get a cat out of a tree, or move a log out the road. Virtually all of the calls to Applebottom's volunteer fire department were inconveniences that citizens really should manage on their own.

He leaned forward and spoke into the intercom. "What is it? Did Betty's dog Clementine take off into the woods again?

"It's an actual fire. Fred's getting the truck."

Micah jumped from his desk, throwing off his suit jacket, and unbuttoning his white dress shirt. "An actual fire? Where?"

"On Murray Street. Linda's place. Upstairs tenant tried to burn something on the lawn."

Micah opened the small wardrobe where he kept his gear and jerked on the pants. "What was she thinking? It's dry as a bone out there."

He didn't bother shutting off the intercom as he snatched up his boots and jacket and hat. He dashed out his door, passing Marianne's desk to plunk down on the chair by the front door. This was going to change his day.

"You want me to reschedule your two o'clock?" Marianne asked.

"Just let him know that I might not make it."

He stomped his feet into his boots. The law office was only four blocks from Murray Street. He could be on the scene on foot faster than anyone else.

"Hold down the fort," Micah said and dashed out the door.

While he half-jogged down the street, he pulled his cell phone out of his pocket and rang Fred.

The man picked up immediately. "You headed there?"

"Yeah I'm only a few blocks away," Micah said. "You got the truck?"

"Opening the doors now. I've got Grant and Jerome headed this way."

"Sounds good. I'll figure out the situation and report."

He hung up and took off in a sprint. He really hoped that the fire was contained to the lawn, but with the grass the way it was, maybe not.

The midsummer sun bore down on Micah as he ran. The small homes were tidy and old-fashioned, the lawns a patchwork. Some—the ones with owners who had decided to hand-water them—were modestly green. Others had given up and let their lawns turn brown and dry.

He had not been down Murray Street in a while. He could only hope that Linda kept her lawn some-what watered, or they were going to have a serious blaze on their hands.

Oh no. Oh no. Oh no.

Lorelei couldn't take her eyes off the fire. What had seemed like a great idea five minutes ago was now clearly her worst ever.

The pile of wadded-up paper, bedding, clothes, and mementos had gone up in flames more swiftly than she would ever have predicted. But then the singed grass of the yard, hot and dry at midsummer, had started smoldering.

Lorelei yelped and dashed for the water hose on the side of the house. But Linda like things neat and organized, and kept the hose rolled up inside a fancy container. By the time Lorelei figured out how to open it and unrolled it long enough to reach the blaze in the front yard, two neighbors had already stepped outside, cell phones in hand.

Lorelei dropped the hose, realizing she had never

turned the water on, and sprinted barefoot to twist the handle. How many stickers were in this grass? Lorelei stumbled and hopped, pain shooting up from her feet. But she had to hurry. What if it got to the house? Her body jangled with panic, and her chest was so tight she was breathless by the time she wrenched open the spigot and dashed around the corner.

By the time she returned to the fire to pick up the hose and start to spray it, she was hobbling.

One of Linda's prize rose bushes near the driveway started smoking. A little darting line of fire had bolted from the pile through the lawn.

This was a disaster.

Arnold, the barber who lived across the street, ran up to her. "What in tarnation were you thinking, setting a fire in the middle of summer? Right here in town?"

"I'm sorry," she said. "I'll put it out. It's not very big."

But the stream of water coming from the hose was puny and weak.

"What's wrong with the water pressure?" Arnold snatched the hose from Lorelei and pressed his thumb to the spray to fan it wider. Where the water landed, it definitely slowed down the fire, but the pile was as big as the bedspread.

"Get back there and turn it up," Arnold shouted.

Lorelei knew she had already turned it as high as

it would go, but she half-hopped, half-limped back to the faucet just to get away from his snarling face. She didn't blame him for being mad. If this went south, it could take out several houses on the street.

Since Arnold was doing everything that could currently be done, she bent over and brushed the stickers off the bottom of her feet. She should have put shoes on before she came downstairs with the candles and the matches.

Her face blazed as hot as her old bedspread. This was the sort of terrible, stupid thing that she'd been known for doing in high school. She would have thought that she'd have gained some common sense in the past six years. But no, when she got upset, it was as though all her brain cells flew out her ears.

"Girl," Arnold shouted, "did you crank up that water?.

She picked her way back to the front lawn, trying to avoid any sticker patches. "It's as high as it goes," she said.

Across the street, the elderly woman who lived next door to Arnold shook her head. "Fred's gettin' the fire truck," she said. "Just make sure it doesn't spread."

"I'm trying!" Arnold shouted back. "I might put this out faster if my Doberman peed on it." He glanced Lorelei's way, took her in from head to toe, and scowled.

Lorelei looked down. *Right.* It was pretty obvious

she had never gotten dressed. She was wearing a sleep tank with the word *diva* printed across it in pink sparkly letters, and polka dot boy shorts.

All her neighbors, some of them in floral house dresses, and others in loose jeans and suspenders, were coming out of their houses.

The retired ones anyway. Although Arnold wasn't retired. What was he doing home in the middle of the afternoon?

Oh, right. It was Monday. His barber shop was closed.

They all stood in the street, watching. She should do something.

"Should I go fill up some containers in the house to pour on it?"

Arnold wouldn't even look her in the eye. His ears had turned red, and his jowls wiggled as he shifted the hose around, trying to get the bedspread wet enough to smother the blaze. Even so, when he sprayed one section, another would zip through the grass, and he'd have to turn his attention to it.

"I think you've done enough," he said, then muttered something else that Lorelei couldn't quite understand. Probably for the best.

She wondered if she could sneak upstairs and change. The only good thing about her predicament at the moment was that nobody was going to take a viral video of her. Not a soul who had come out to gawk had a cell phone in the air, taking the telltale video or live broadcast. But the Applebottom gossip mill? She'd definitely be the equivalent of viral on *that*.

She wasn't sure which was worse.

Several heads turned up the street at the same time. Lorelei followed their gazes to see what was more interesting than her front yard blaze.

It was definitely worth a look. A dark-haired firefighter, partially dressed in yellow gear, ran full speed up the street.

It didn't take long for her to recognize him. Micah Livingston. Her stomach flipped. He'd been every girl's crush at Applebottom High School back in the day, even though Lorelei had only been a seventh grader when he graduated. He was one of those dreamy good-looking boys who dressed sharp and knew just how to sweet-talk a girl.

And he could be wild. Lorelei's older sister Mandy had told some pretty crazy stories about the basketball players and the parties they would throw at the Livingston house when Micah's family was traveling.

She hadn't seen him around town much since she'd returned, demoralized and jobless after dropping out of college. She hadn't wanted to go back and live with her parents, so she rented the space above Linda's house. At least until her last college loan ran out.

Micah was a lawyer now, though, she knew that

much. And he obviously did some firefighting on the side.

As he approached, she took in the white T-shirt beneath the suspenders that held up the fire pants. He held his jacket under one arm, his hat beneath the other. As he approached the blaze, he put his hat on his head. He'd grown a light beard since she last saw him.

He passed right by her and ran up to Arnold, who was still wielding the wimpy hose.

"That all the pressure you got?"

"She claims she turned it all the way up," Arnold said, aiming a thumb in Lorelei's direction.

Micah donned his jacket and pulled on a pair of gloves. He walked right into the middle of the burning bedspread and shifted it until it lay flat over the burning pile. "Get the rest of it wet," he said.

Within seconds, the wet blanket had smothered the flames.

A siren sounded from a few blocks down, and the red fire truck roared up the street.

The neighbors all clapped for Micah as Lorelei shrank farther back against the wall of Linda's house. Maybe now was the time to make her inconspicuous exit, at least to put on some different clothes. She knew they were going to want to talk to her, and she'd rather not have to face the mob in her pajama shorts.

But just as she was about to slip inside the house,

Micah turned and saw her. His penetrating gaze stopped her in her tracks.

She felt imprisoned, unable to move.

"Is that the girl who started it?" he asked Arnold, not taking his eyes off her.

"That would be the one," Arnold said.

"She from around here?"

Lorelei puffed with indignation. Pretending not to know a born-and-bred citizen of Applebottom was pretty much the biggest insult you could make in this town.

She stomped right up to him, refusing to wince when her bare foot landed on another cluster of stickers. "Micah Livingston, you know good and well that I'm Lorelei Spencer. You went to high school with my sister Mandy."

Micah's eyebrows shot up. "You're little Lori? The spunky snot-nosed kid who used to steal cupcakes out of Mandy's lunch?"

This was all he remembered about her?

She couldn't come up with a witty reply. "I don't even like cupcakes," she said defiantly.

The small crowd broke into light laughter. Right. Who doesn't like cupcakes? She probably looked as silly as she had when she got caught with her hand in Mandy's lunchbox in elementary school.

Micah's eyes were on her, though, and she had to hold her ground.

Nobody made fun of Lorelei Spencer, not even a hottie smarty-pants lawyer.

❧

One thing was clear. Micah had made little Lorelei mad.

She stood, not four feet from him, her fist on one hip, which jutted angrily to one side in polka dot shorts.

Micah didn't know if this was the sort of outfit Lorelei wore all the time, but it looked more like something you would sleep in, rather than an outfit for setting a mid-afternoon fire on your front lawn.

The red-and-blue lights of the fire truck crossed their faces during their standoff, until Fred climbed down and walked over.

"Looks like you got this one contained pretty quick," he said.

Micah tore his gaze from Lorelei. She definitely wasn't the same little scamp he remembered.

"We just wet down the blanket," he told Fred. He tilted his head at the barber, who still held the water hose. "Arnold here did some quick thinking and kept it from spreading."

Fred lifted his fire hat and scratched his scruffy, half-bald head. His watery blue eyes shifted around, surveying the spectators, the pile—then his gaze paused on Lorelei.

Micah held back his grin. Fred was about to give Lorelei a piece of his mind. He was famous for it.

"Somebody want to inform me about how this got started?" he asked.

Lorelei shifted on her bare feet. She cast her eyes down, and the defiant stance disappeared.

"I did it," she said. "I wasn't thinking. I was just trying to get rid of some stuff I didn't want around anymore."

"You know, open burning during summer isn't exactly a safe move," Fred said. "You could've put a lot of people and houses in danger."

"I see that." Lorelei still stared at the ground like a chastised child.

"You know, it's actually a crime," Fred said. "You could be arrested."

At that, Lorelei's head popped up. "Oh, no. Please don't call Officer Stone."

Fred kicked the corner of the charred bedspread. "What's all this stuff?"

Lorelei lunged forward. "I'll clean it all up," she blurted. "Don't worry. I'll get it. I'm really sorry."

Micah bent down and scooped up a notebook that was only slightly damaged. Loopy handwriting on the front cover read *Our Best Moments Together*.

Lorelei snatched the notebook from his hands. "It's nothing."

Fred knocked aside more of the bedspread. A

jumble of soggy blackened paper, stuffed animals, and a hunk of misshapen wax lay beneath.

A couple of the sodden pages had hearts all over them. Micah caught sight of the words *love, forever,* and *sweetheart.* He was starting to get a picture of what happened here. A relationship had ended, and Lorelei wanted to destroy all the evidence.

The small crowd that had gathered scooted in closer, also curious about what had started the whole thing.

Micah cleared his throat. "We have this under control. Everybody can go on back now. We'll get it cleaned up."

Lorelei sank to her knees in the mud, gathering up any of the pages that were still legible. Micah turned to Fred. "I'm gonna stay here and help her get this picked up and make sure nothing else has a hotspot," he said. "You can take the truck on back. We're good."

Fred looked between the two of them for a moment and gave him an exaggerated wink. "I'll have the boys clear everybody out," he said.

While Fred and a couple of his volunteers shooed everyone back to their houses, Micah moved the singed blanket off the pile and began tossing the debris onto it.

"This'll make it quicker to pick up," he said to Lorelei, who had gathered a significant chunk of pages against her chest. She was muddy now from ankle to knee, and her clothes were covered in soot. Her straw-colored hair was twisted into a little knot on top of her head, random tendrils falling all around.

She looked ridiculously cute, a smudge on her nose, the papers clutched in her arms.

He shifted a little closer. "We can take this directly out to the dump, if you're worried the neighbors might get nosy in the trash bin."

"They would do that?"

"Murray Street is known for its retirees who don't have much to do."

Her eyes teared over. Micah wondered if this was a pretty recent breakup. That would explain all the crazy emotions and acting without thought.

"Let's get it all off the ground." Micah chucked his hat and the heavy gear to start gathering the debris.

Lorelei picked up something that might once have been a skirt and began folding papers and notebooks into it. Those probably had the most personal stuff in them.

Micah understood. He'd been pretty broken up over a girl a few years back. Back in law school, he'd met Angelique, and they'd gotten pretty tight. She came from big money, and both her parents and his were thrilled with the match.

He'd planned to propose to her as soon as he passed the bar exam. His intention then was to find a large firm in a major market, a place where he could move up and become partner.

The two of them loved big city living, museums and opera and nightlife. A large crew, mostly law students and some random friends, threw parties and took over restaurants.

It was quite the experience, and Micah loved it.

Then life back in Applebottom crashed.

His little brother Joshua was stationed in Iraq and his tanker hit an incendiary device. He'd been killed instantly.

When Micah had come home for the funeral, his parents were mere shells of the vibrant couple they once had been. He thought they'd recover with time, but when they showed up at his law school graduation a year later, little had changed. His father admitted that he hadn't kept up with his caseload. His mother took him aside and asked what his intentions were when he passed the bar, because he was really needed at home.

The answer became clear. At least for a while, Micah would take over his father's firm.

This decision did not sit well with Angelique. She asked him to think on the decision for a while before dooming them to that sad little town.

But he started going home more often to check on his parents—and also to mourn Josh in his own way, hanging out in the places where they had grown up together. He found he couldn't leave, and when his bar results came in, he assured his father that he was ready to take over.

The cases were in terrible disarray, and it had taken him another year just to get a handle on everything that had been neglected.

By then, his parents had started jet-setting around the globe, seeming to think that if they stayed away from Applebottom they could forget what they had lost.

Angelique quit visiting. Micah ended up rattling around in his parents' enormous lake house until he bought a small place a couple blocks off Town Square.

Work had been Micah's salvation. He'd not only taken over all of his father's cases, but also added many of his own. He might not be a big city lawyer, but he definitely had the work ethic. He was trusted by all the members of his community, and that was important to him.

"Can you help me with this?" Lorelei asked.

Micah shook loose from his past to see Lorelei struggling with more melted wax, which had cooled and sealed several stuffed animals into a clump of dead grass.

Together they tugged until it tore free of the ground. Micah took it from her and tossed it on the bedspread with the other things.

The street had emptied out, the onlookers all back

in their homes. Fred had driven off with the truck and crew.

It was just the two of them.

"Thanks for your help," she said, as they rolled the corners of the bedspread on top of the pile.

"I can bring my truck around if you want me to haul it for you," he said. "I ran here from my office since my house was the wrong direction, but it's not far."

She looked it over. "I think it will fit in my trunk. Let me get my keys."

She ran inside the house and her bare feet thumped on the wood steps. Micah stood over the pile.

The wind picked up and blew a couple balled-up pieces of paper from an open edge. Micah chased them down and scooped them up. The words jumped out at him.

He called me babe today. Does this mean I'm a babe? His babe?

I'll always be his babe. Forever. He is my one true love.

Micah glanced at the upstairs window, still open. Lorelei passed by it but didn't look out.

He folded the pages and tucked them under a corner of the blanket.

Tough times for Lorelei. He understood that.

Three days after Lorelei's now-infamous fire, she was still hearing daily rants from her landlord.

At first Linda had insisted she move out, but the other ladies in Linda's quilting circle—including Lorelei's mother, Mary—convinced her not to be so drastic. After all, no harm had been done, and the grass couldn't have gotten any more dead than it already was.

Honestly, Lorelei was surprised that her mother had come to her defense. She'd been trying to get Lorelei to move back home ever since she dropped out of the University of Arkansas.

Seven months had passed since then, and Lorelei knew she couldn't keep living this way. The loan originally intended to cover her final semester had been stretched due to how much she saved by living in Applebottom, plus not having tuition. But come September, the money would run out, and she would be expected to start paying off the loan.

Laurel laughed a little. As if that could happen.

It wasn't that she sat at home and did nothing. She had a little online craft store where she made love charms, tiny bracelets with hearts and gemstones and miniature potion bottles that were meant to bring young women luck with relationships.

They were pretty popular, actually, and she spent a couple hours a day filling orders. She'd just never really gotten a handle on exactly how much she ought to charge, and even in the months where she sold a lot of bracelets, she couldn't seem to get very far ahead.

Lorelei flopped back on her Hello Kitty bedspread. She was due to hang out with her girl-friends from high school, Bethany and Candace, but she hadn't been too motivated to get ready.

Bethany was married and pregnant. And Candace dressed like a runway model, making Lorelei's wardrobe look like dumpster rejects.

Still, it was something to do. And an escape from Linda.

She got up and started sorting through her closet, noticeably emptier now that she'd tossed everything she associated with Gary. Great. Even less to choose from. She picked a pair of newish jeans and a plain cotton shirt, and headed to the bathroom.

Lorelei was supremely grateful that she had an older sister—one who'd done all the right things, like going to college and actually finishing. Mandy had found a proper husband in the process, getting married in a big hometown wedding and having a baby two years later.

This took an immense amount of pressure off Lorelei. She was perfectly fine with being the screw-up daughter. Trouble in high school. Dropping out of college.

Now setting fire to the lawn.

Her phone buzzed. Thank goodness her parents still made that payment, or she probably wouldn't even have one anymore. She picked it up to read the text.

It was a notification that she had a whopper order. Eighty bracelets!

Lorelei let out a little whoop. That would cover rent for a month. She hoped she had enough supplies.

She danced a little jig by the sink, her toothbrush hanging out of her mouth. Her luck had turned around today.

§

By the time Lorelei walked into Annabelle's Café, Bethany and Candace were already there, sitting in a corner by the jukebox.

Bethany stood up to give her a long squeezy hug,

her barely-there baby belly pushed out to the fullest to make sure everybody noticed.

"Look at that bump!" Lorelei squealed. "Your baby is growing!"

"So is my butt," Bethany said, turning around to look down at her still very normal-sized backend. "I'm going to end up as big as a house."

Candace stayed in her seat. She swung her sleek ebony hair behind her shoulder and gave a wan smile. Huh. She looked to be in a mood.

As Bethany and Lorelei settled in their chairs, Flo, the white-haired waitress who'd been serving there since before Lorelei was born, walked up.

"Water, tea or soda?" she asked Lorelei.

"Sweet tea for me," Lorelei said. She turned to her friends. "I'm feeling fancy because I just got a huge bracelet order."

"Yay!" Bethany said. "Does this mean you can put off having to move back in with the fam?"

"One more month at least."

Candace fiddled with the lemon wedge stuck on the rim of her water glass. She no longer drank sweet tea because sugar was "white death," though she didn't say it out loud in places like Annabelle's Café. Those were fightin' words.

"So you're really not going back to U of A?" she asked.

Lorelei deflated a bit. "I might finish sometime. My grades were in the toilet, and I definitely wasn't going to get a job in English literature even if I did finish."

She'd only started that major because she loved to read and at the time, she'd had a serious crush on a devastatingly cute English teacher at Applebottom high school.

"You could probably get your teaching degree with all that English you already have," Candace said. She taught third grade at the elementary.

"Oh, no. I'm hopeless with kids."

Bethany patted her belly. "I bet you change your mind once you have your own. I'm already in love with this little guy."

The beginning of a headache started pulsing in Lorelei's temple. Normally her friends weren't ones to preach at her.

The waitress bought Lorelei's tea and they each placed their orders. Lorelei was feeling flush after her mega order, so instead of getting the cheapest thing on the menu, she ordered a burger and fries and a slice of apple pie.

After the waitress left, no one said anything, and Lorelei looked from Bethany to Candace and back. Something was definitely up.

"What?" Lorelei asked.

Bethany took the bait. "We heard that you left out a small detail about your little fire a few days ago."

"What are you talking about? I told you I finally tossed all of Gary's things."

"We mean about your white knight in a firefighter uniform," Bethany said. "Micah Livingston. The lawyer. Pretty much the most eligible bachelor in Applebottom."

Lorelei picked up her tea and took a sip. "Oh. Him."

Bethany leaned forward, making sure her belly was tucked beneath the table edge. "We heard he helped you clean everything up and even used his truck to take it all to the dump."

Lorelei had left that part out of her texts to her friends. "Now see, I just knew you would make a big deal out of it. It was no skin off his back. My stuff just didn't fit in my trunk."

Candace's perfectly arched eyebrows lifted an inch. "So he conveniently drove you?"

"It meant nothing!" Lorelei insisted. "He's a member of the volunteer fire department. It's his job to help citizens in distress."

"And you are definitely Applebottom's most distressed citizen," Candace said. "You're one month away from moving back in with your parents. You have no plans. Girl, what are you going to do?"

"I'm gonna sit here and eat a cheeseburger that I paid for with the work of my own two hands," Lorelei said, realizing she sounded like a six-year-old. "And nothing else happened with Micah. We drove down to the dump, and we drove back. In fact, he acted like he didn't even know who I was when he showed up to the fire."

"Now, that's not okay," Bethany said.

"I know!" Lorelei said, her voice rising to the point that a couple other patrons at the diner turned to look.

She hunched down in her seat. "That's just all I mean. To him I'm still some snotty nosed brat out to steal a cupcake."

"A what?" Candace asked.

"Nevermind. Just don't get all excited. Nothing can happen between me and Micah Livingston."

They all chatted about other things until a man cleared his throat behind Lorelei's chair. She whipped around.

The deputy stood there all formal-like, his hands clasped behind his back.

Candace's voice was so sharp, it could have cut glass. "Can we help you, Jeremy?"

Candace had actually dated Jeremy for a while in high school. There was no love lost between those two. And she had zero respect for the fact that he was now an officer of the law.

"Hello, Lorelei," he said. "Hey, Bethany." He paused and looked at his ex. "Candace."

"What do you want?" Candace snapped.

Jeremy rocked back on his heels. He was tall and muscled in his khaki uniform. He adjusted his hat and presented a brown envelope to Lorelei. "This is official business. Judge Hughes sent me down with this for you, Lorelei."

Lorelei felt a shiver go all the way from her shoulders to her toes. Why would Jeremy be bringing her something in person?

"What is it?" she asked, her voice wavering.

"I don't have liberty to say," Jeremy said. "I was just instructed to serve you this officially and in person. Can you sign here?"

He produced a clipboard.

"Don't sign anything," Candace said. "He can't make you sign."

Jeremy tapped the blank line next to Lorelei's name with a pen. "I reckon I can try," he said, his voice calm, "given that this here is an official document from the Applebottom Court."

Bethany slid the envelope closer to her. "Is this a summons?" she asked. "Johnny got one just like it when he had to go in for a speeding ticket."

"I'm not at liberty to say," Jeremy said again.

"What happens if I don't sign?" Lorelei asked.

"Doesn't change a thing," Jeremy said. "I just make a note that the recipient refused to sign, but it doesn't take away from the fact that the document was, in fact, served."

Lorelei took the pen and scrawled her name on the line. She'd never been in any kind of trouble before. Not even a parking ticket. She looked up at Jeremy. "How did you know I was here?"

"When I went to your place, Linda called your mama. Your mama called your grandma Betty, who said Bethany had been in the tea shop yesterday saying she was going to be meeting you for lunch today." His eyes glanced off Bethany, dropping to her belly, then back to Lorelei. "I checked in with Annabelle, and she confirmed the three of you were right here. Seemed as good a time as any to drop by."

"In front of everybody," Lorelei hissed.

"Does this have to do with that fire you set?" Bethany asked, her voice hushed now, too.

"Surely not," Lorelei said, her heart really starting to hammer. She looked up at Jeremy. "Does it?"

"I'm not at –"

"At liberty to say," Lorelei interrupted. "Got it."

"Well, open it," Bethany said.

Jeremy picked up his clipboard as if to leave, but Candace stopped him cold.

"You stay right there, Jeremy Banks."

Jeremy's mouth opened for a moment, then closed. But he didn't move.

Several people at tables nearby had started to stare. Lorelei closed her eyes for a moment, trying to gather her composure. Then she slid her finger underneath the flap of the envelope and pried it open.

Inside were several pieces of paper. She quickly scanned the top one.

Lorelei Spencer is hereby summoned to court on 4

August at 10:30 AM on the matter of the violation of Ordinance 14 Part B of the fire code.

"What is it?" Bethany asked. "Tell us!"

Lorelei wanted to throw up. "It's the fire. I have to go to court."

Bethany's hand fluttered to her chest. "Are you under arrest?"

They all looked up at Jeremy.

"I'm just here to serve the document," he said. "No arrest."

They all breathed a little easier. Candace shooed him away, and they huddled over the pages.

"You have to get a lawyer," Candace said.

"How am I going to afford a lawyer?" Lorelei cried.

"What about your hero the fireman?" Candace asked.

"I don't know. Would he?" Lorelei's head buzzed. This was terrible. She could barely afford her rent!

This was the worst disaster of her life.

CHAPTER 4

Micah shook the hands of the Brown family and began clearing his paperwork and folders from the table. The courtroom had emptied. Finalizing the division of this contentious estate had taken a good part of the afternoon.

Judge Hughes stood up from behind his podium and stretched. "Micah, can I see you in my chambers when you've gathered everything?"

That was odd. Micah glanced up at the man. Judge Hughes's fine gray hair tufted up in the air conditioning. He was already unzipping the front of his robe.

"Sure. Is everything okay?"

"Oh, yes, of course. I just need your help on a little matter."

"I'll be right there."

Micah had shoved most of the folders in his valise

when a tug at the bottom of his suit jacket drew his attention downward. Melody, the youngest grand-daughter of the late Mr. Brown, looked up at him with her clear blue eyes and sweet five-year-old face.

"This is for you," she said, and held up a white sheet of paper covered in a crayon depiction of the courtroom. Judge Hughes sat behind his big rectangle. And Micah was drawn sitting behind the table.

"Why thank you, Melody." Micah smiled at the girl and accepted the piece of paper. "You did a really good job."

Micah glanced up to see Melody's mother at the back of the courtroom, scowling. She definitely wasn't behind the picture, and looked impatient for this moment to end. She hadn't gotten what she wanted. Micah had to uphold the will, even though her lawyer had attempted to argue around it.

The girl skipped off down the aisle and took her mother's hand. Micah tucked the drawing among the other papers on the case and shoved them in his briefcase.

He was glad to have that probate done. It was always hardest when the family bickered among themselves. Micah found it much easier to deal with cases with more objective divisions to be made. Stocks, bonds, debt payoff, company ownership to be split.

He grabbed his valise by the handle and headed to

the back exit of the courtroom toward the judge's chamber. The bailiff gave him a nod and allowed him back.

The judge sat on a chair in one corner, his robe draped over the back. He pulled off his tie. "Micah, come in."

Micah sat near him. Judge Hughes hadn't called him to his chambers since Micah first started managing his father's cases. That time, the judge had taken him aside to make sure he was able to take on the chaos of work.

"I've sat on this bench for almost twenty-five years," the judge said.

Micah shifted in his seat. The sounded like the opening of a lengthy lecture.

"I've done a few favors from this bench," the judge went on, "as long as I thought they were fair and a good idea." He paused, folding his hands together. "And I reckon I'll do this new one. It involves you."

"Okay," Micah said. "What is it?"

"Technically it's a criminal matter, but I'm going to make it a civil one to keep it simple."

Micah laughed. "How can creating a civil dispute ever make something simpler?"

"Fair point," the judge said. "But I'd rather not affect anybody's criminal record." He rubbed his chin.

Micah leaned forward. "Now you have me curious. What's going on?"

"You remember that girl Lorelei Spencer?"

Oh, that. Micah briefly wondered if he had violated some code of ethics by helping her after the fire, or by sending Fred away. "I do. She tried burning some trash in the yard and got in a bit of trouble."

"Yes. Well, it seems that some of our citizens want to make sure she thinks before she does something like that again."

"Are they going to charge her with arson? Public endangerment? Criminal mischief?"

"No, no. I want to keep it a civil matter, remember."

Micah sat back in the chair. "Right."

"She's been summoned to court in a couple weeks," he said.

"Is Linda behind this? I hope you're not listening to her."

"Now, let's not speak ill of poor Linda," Judge Hughes said. "She wouldn't be the first elderly person to get a little contentious in her later years. I'm probably heading that way myself." He laughed a little. "Here's the rub. I'm going to bring Lorelei in to court. And I want you to represent her."

Micah sat up straight. "I don't do that kind of case. I don't know anything about defending a person from whatever you're going to do."

"That's why it's a civil case."

"That's still way out of my wheelhouse," Micah insisted.

"This is a personal favor to me," the judge said. "I'll

steer you through it. The girl's going to be really anxious now that she's been served, and since you two have already gotten acquainted, you're the best person to help her out." He picked up a brown packet of papers and passed them over.

Micah knew when he was being strong-armed. "All right," he said, tucking the packet in his valise. "I don't figure I have the option of saying no, anyway."

The judge chuckled. "Now you understand. Jeremy served her at Annabelle's Café at lunchtime."

"I bet that went over like a lead balloon."

"He said she was a little freaked out." Judge Hughes stood and stretched out his hand. "I'd go see her sooner rather than later. She could use a little guidance."

Micah clasped the older man's hand. "I'll do my best."

He picked up his valise and headed out of the chambers. He had no idea what to do with this case, or even what to expect at the hearing. But he had a packet full of papers to read about it, and maybe it was time for him to branch out a little.

Time to go see Lorelei.

CHAPTER 5

*T*onight was definitely a night to be a *paper shaker.*

Lorelei twisted the last lock of loose hair around an orange juice can and meticulously pinned it in place. She'd learned the technique from her grandmother Betty, who still did wet sets at the beauty parlor every Friday afternoon. When Lorelei was a little girl, and at odds with her own mother, she would ride her bike over to Grandma Betty's and they would transform themselves into paper shakers, a term from the 1950s for cheerleaders.

It was one of Grandma Betty's favorite expressions, along with *classy chassis* and *cut a rug.* Both of which apparently defined her teen years.

They would set their hair with pin curls for tight curls or orange juice cans for loose. Grandma Betty would drag out a funny little blow dryer with the tube that snaked into a plastic bonnet. When she turned it on, Lorelei's entire head felt warm and protected.

Grandma Betty would drag out poodle skirts and a couple pairs of well-worn black and white saddle shoes. The two of them would have a sock hop around the living room after their curls were set, listening to Nat King Cole and Buddy Holly and Elvis Presley.

The old hairdryer head given up the ghost a decade ago, but sometimes when Lorelei was particularly blue, she would still pin up her hair and dance around the room to Elvis.

She couldn't crank the music like at Grandma Betty's house, as Linda got sore pretty easily if Lorelei was noisy. But these days, Lorelei had earbuds, and she could listen to the playlist as much as she wanted all by herself.

The poodle skirts and saddle shoes were still at her grandmother's, but Lorelei could evoke the same feeling in her pink shorty baby-doll pajamas and fuzzy robe. She wore matching feathery slippers with a kitten heel and blew a kiss at herself in the bathroom mirror as she passed.

With thick black eyeliner and bright red lips, she looked like a retro ad for vacuum cleaners, or maybe soda pop. She shook her imaginary pom poms to "Jailhouse Rock" and tried to blank her mind from the packet of papers Jeremy had delivered in front of everybody at Annabelle's Café.

There it was again. Her problems. She twirled in a circle, trying to evade the thoughts, and put an extra wiggle in her hips as the song wound down to its conclusion.

Only in the dead space between songs did she hear the knock at the door.

Crud. It was probably Linda, here to try and evict her again since she was a hardened criminal.

She could *ignore* the knock. It might be her mother, about to drive her home for the same reason. Probably only her grandmother would be sympathetic to her situation. Lorelei glanced at the clock. It was after six. Grandma Betty would have closed up her tea shop hours ago. Lorelei should probably call her, if for no other reason than to get a heads-up on the state of her parents.

The knock came again, insistent. Lorelei checked that her hair was still securely tucked around the orange juice cans and pulled the earbuds out. Fine. Might as well see who was here to give her grief.

She flung the door open, then took two steps back in surprise.

It was the firefighter, Micah. The one who remembered how she used to steal Mandy's cupcakes. He looked completely put together in khaki pants and a crisp short-sleeved sea-green polo. He could have just stepped off a yacht.

Lorelei's face flamed. "What are you doing here?"

Micah's eyebrows rose in surprise as he took in her outfit. "Why are you always in sleepwear?"

Lorelei wrapped her robe around her body, not that it helped that much. Neither the shorty pajamas or the robe fell even halfway down her thigh.

"I'm paper shaking. It's what I wear."

Micah shook his head in confusion. "Paper what?"

"Never mind," she said. "Am I in more trouble?" She pictured herself in handcuffs in her pink baby-doll and orange juice rollers, and got lightheaded.

"No. I'm not the police."

Right. he was a lawyer. "Okay," she said. "Can I help you then?"

"I'm very curious about this, what did you call it?" Micah leaned against the door.

"Paper shaking," she said. "It's a term from the 50s. For cheerleaders. You know, pom poms?" She shook her fists as if she were holding a set.

"Oh," he said with a nod. "I get it."

"What did you say you needed?" Lorelei was fit to be tied. She really wanted some pants. She glanced down. Oh, those the peep-toe furry kitten heeled shoes. Her face felt like it might explode from embarrassment.

Micah grinned like he'd just spiked the punch at prom. "I was here to see if you wanted to chat about the notice that you got from Judge Hughes."

Lorelei stared at the floor as she composed herself

and finally said, "Does everybody in the whole town know about that?"

"Probably," he said. "Judge Hughes called me and asked if I would take your case."

What? Lorelei snapped her head up. Micah? Helping her?

"Really?"

"It's not the sort of case I normally handle, but Judge Hughes felt that I was the best person to represent you at the hearing. Do you want my help?"

"Well, yes!" Lorelei stumbled back a few steps. "Of course I do. That would be amazing." She shifted aside to give him room to pass. "Come in. I guess I need details. How much would it cost? I'm really broke. But I just sold a lot of bracelets, so I would probably have a down payment. Could I pay you like a hundred dollars now?"

Micah stepped into her room, and immediately it felt small. And pink.

He glanced around, quirking a smile as his eyes fell on random objects. She viewed the room from his perspective: the Hello Kitty bedspread, her collection of unicorn buttons pinned to a long satin ribbon, and the giant framed wall portrait of young Elvis over her bed. She must seem like a total child.

"I got the impression that I was doing this pro bono," Micah said, "so you don't need to worry about paying me. It's a pretty simple matter."

He stood in the center of the room, arms crossed,

and Lorelei realized she had lost her manners. She rushed over to her desk to pull out the rolling chair. "Sorry. Sit here," she said.

She sat on the corner of her bed, then leapt up like it was on fire when she realized she had just sat on her bed in shorty pajamas, while alone in a room with the town lawyer.

She tried to casually lean against the wall instead.

"You take the chair," Micah said. "I've been sitting all day."

"Actually, I have another one," Lorelei said, dashing across the room to the white metal chair that matched her vanity table. She dragged it over and plunked down in it. She folded her fuzzy robe over her knees. There. That was better. She felt more covered.

"So the juice cans in your hair are for..." Micah began.

"Oh," Lorelei said, her hands flying to her head. "It's just a way of setting curls. An old-fashioned way. Grandma Betty taught it to me."

"That's right, Betty is your grandmother." His expression shifted, and his thumb tapped his perfectly pressed trouser at his knee. "You know, this is starting to make sense. Judge Hughes is a big fan of your grandmother. I bet she put him up to having me do this."

Oh. So he hadn't *wanted* to help her. "You don't

have to," Lorelei said. "I mean, I need you, but I don't want to force you or anything."

"No, it's fine," Micah said. "I didn't mean to suggest that I didn't want to help you. I'm just putting the pieces together about how all this came about."

"How did it?" Lorelei asked. "I was gobsmacked when I got that notice. I thought when Fred left with the fire truck that it was over."

"Me too," Micah said. "Normally this would be a criminal charge."

Lorelei sucked in a breath. "Like I did it on purpose?"

"Well, didn't you?"

"I didn't mean to set the lawn on fire! I just wanted to get rid of my stuff."

Micah held up a hand. "I know. I get it. It's fine. The judge has made this a civil matter. This is a more manageable case for him and doesn't go on your criminal record."

Lorelei looked down at her hands. "I see. It was a really dumb thing I did, wasn't it?"

"I think we've been over that," Micah said. "But sometimes people going through a bad breakup do things without thinking."

Lorelei couldn't look him in the eye. The last thing she wanted to do was talk about Gary.

"Was it recent?" Micah asked gently.

"Not really," she said. "About a year."

Micah shifted in his chair, and Lorelei glanced a

little higher, almost afraid to see his expression. Was he going to judge her over this?

She spoke in a rush. "I know I should've gotten over him a long time ago. It was just one of those things. I thought he was the one. But he wasn't."

"I know exactly what you mean," Micah said.

"You do? I mean, of course you do. Although, really? Someone broke up with *you*?"

Micah tilted his head. "Does that seem so crazy?"

"No, no," she stammered. "I mean, well, maybe. I mean, you're like perfect. Nice. A lawyer. Handsome."

Oh, *shut up*, Lorelei!

Micah chuckled. "I don't think I'm particularly perfect."

"This town thinks you are," Lorelei said. "My mom thinks you walk on water. My dad, too. Didn't you date like every girl in my sister's class?"

"I don't think so," Micah said. "I never dated your sister. How is she, anyway? I don't see her around town much."

"Oh, you know. Little Shila is barely three plus there's another one on the way. She's got her hands full."

"Must make your family happy, having those little ones around."

Lorelei's hands flew in the air in excitement, and she reined them in, dropping them back in her lap. "Oh, of course. And I love it. Because of them, no one bothers me about husbands and babies. My sister did everything right. Every single thing right."

The words echoed in the room until it was quiet.

"I see," Micah said. "Well, let's go over what can happen. Are you okay with talking in here?"

Lorelei sat up straight. "Why wouldn't I be?"

Micah opened his mouth and closed it, then opened it again. "I mean, did you want to change or go somewhere more public?"

Lorelei looked down. Right. She was in shorty pajamas with juice cans in her hair and a man in her room.

"Just give me two minutes," she said, jumping up. "I'll put on regular clothes and take down my hair."

"I think it's cute," Micah said. "I just wanted to give you an option."

Lorelei practically sprinted into the bathroom. "Two minutes!"

She slammed the door, then leaned against it. She was blowing this in every way possible.

Micah Livingston was in her bedroom. Even stoic Candace, who didn't bat an eyelash at anybody, called him the most eligible bachelor in Applebottom.

Here. With *her*.

Lorelei turned to the mirror.

She did look pretty doggone cute.

Micah waited on the desk chair in Lorelei's bedroom, piecing together a little bit more about the woman from the surroundings.

There was no particular color scheme to the room — pink and white Hello Kitty bedding, gold curtains, a mix of throw pillows in every shade. Lorelei did keep it tidy, though.

He swiveled in his chair to face the desk. This was covered with little trinkets. Charms and lockets and bits of metal, hoops and clasps. A clear plastic shelving unit held every manner of colored beads. A few pieces of jewelry had been strung together on a mat, although none of them appeared to be finished. One was blue wire strung with stars and moons and the tiniest pale green bottle. He nudged it with his finger. Carefully painted on one side were the words *love potion*. It even had a minuscule cork.

This must be the bracelet order she was referring to earlier. Was that what she did to support herself?

He didn't know much about her. She would've been more his brother Josh's age. In a town as small as Applebottom, you generally knew everybody. And although he was aware of her as Mandy's baby sister, he definitely never ran around in her crowd.

Lorelei's shadow changed the pattern of light coming through the bottom of the bathroom door as she walked around. A drawer thumped. Something clattered on the counter.

He smiled to himself. She'd been pretty adorable in that get up. And the rollers. When he'd first seen her, he wondered if she was doing a photo shoot for some sort of retro magazine. She looked that perfect.

The door creaked, and Lorelei emerged, looking considerably more twenty-first century in jeans and a short-sleeved T-shirt that read *fancy*.

Her lips were more subdued now, although she left the eyeliner. It suited her. Her hair fell in soft loose waves.

"Did the rollers do that?" he asked.

She touched her hair. "Yes." Her eyes darted away as though she were embarrassed by the whole thing.

"I thought we'd head to the library," Micah said. "It's open late tonight, and there are tons of tables where we can spread out. Do you have the papers Jeremy served?"

"Yes," she said, lunging for the table by her bed. She picked up a large envelope and tucked it under her elbow. "Anything else I need to bring?"

"I don't think so," he said. "We'll probably end up meeting more than once, so anything else we need, we can revisit at a later date."

They walked out into the hall and headed down the stairs. It was a direct shot to the front door, giving both Lorelei and Linda a small amount of privacy.

"Do you guys share the kitchen?" Micah asked as they stepped outside.

Lorelei turned to lock the front door. "Not really. If I want to cook something big, I can mention it, and she'll give me access to the main kitchen. But there's a second room upstairs that's mine, and it has hot plate and a microwave and a little table to eat at. It works well enough."

"Do you want to take my truck or just walk?" Micah asked.

"It's only a few blocks," Lorelei said. "If you can run it in firefighter gear, I'm sure we can walk it."

They headed down the sidewalk. The night was balmy. It had hit ninety degrees that day.

"Sure are a lot of stars out," Lorelei said. Her face turned up to the sky. "I intended to take astronomy in college so I could learn all the constellations. It just never happened."

"Where did you go?" Mike asked.

"University of Arkansas," she said. "I almost finished. I just had a semester left."

"What happened?"

She hesitated, as if she didn't really want to tell the story. Then she said, "The breakup. I had it in my head how everything was going to fall out. Gary and I would graduate side-by-side, or at least sitting on the same row. He was a Springer and I was a Spencer, and they do it alphabetically. Then he'd do something crazy like propose on stage, and everyone would laugh and throw their hats. He'd get a job. I would use my English degree to do I don't know what. Be a secretary I guess, until I was needed at home to raise some littles."

"And then it all fell apart," he said. He was trying not to judge her, but letting another person derail you so hard that you end up dropping out of school seemed a bit much.

"I don't know," she said. "I started questioning everything. My major. My degree. My plan. I quit going to class. My grades fell. I just didn't want to waste the money on another semester until I figured stuff out."

Their shoes crunched on loose gravel as they crossed the street toward Town Square. They passed Delilah, who was walking her bulldog Bruno, and waved. She'd probably just locked up her doggy bakery.

When Delilah was well behind them, Lorelei let out a groan. "I'm sure she's going to immediately call my mama or my grandma," Lorelei said. "There goes your idiot daughter who set fire to Applebottom and now she's got to meet with a lawyer."

"It's okay," Micah said. "This will pass."

"I keep thinking I'll get my life together, and it just doesn't happen."

"You'll figure it out. Sometimes you're headed one direction, and life just sends you in a different one."

She gave him a sidelong glance. "And what do you know about that, Micah Livingston, son of some of the richest people in Applebottom, taking over your father's business, always knowing what you're going to do and where you're going to do it?"

"You keep saying that," Micah said. "I think you might be forgetting that our family took quite a turn a few years ago, and it reset everybody's priorities."

Now Lorelei look chagrined. She picked at a piece of fluff on her shirt. "I'm so sorry," she said. "I was awful sad to hear about Josh. I was a freshman at U of A when it happened. Mandy called and told me."

"I didn't really intend to come back to Applebottom," Micah said. "But I had to adjust my priorities and do what needed to be done."

"Where were you going instead?"

"I had no idea. I was about to graduate and take

the bar exam, and hoping some great offers would come my way. I certainly didn't picture myself back here. But it's been a good move. I don't resent it."

"Well, I sure do," Lorelei said. "Every day I wish I'd done something different. Gone somewhere else. I can't even mail a letter in this town without somebody looking over my shoulder to see who it's to."

They came to the square and turned in front of the pie shop. The inside was all dark, the doors locked up for the day.

"This town sure shuts down early," Lorelei said with a sigh. She peered into Arnold's barbershop as they passed. "You can't even get a haircut past six o'clock."

"That's how it works with small town businesses," Micah said. "They want to get home to their families."

"Six o'clock is when the day really begins!"

Micah had no comment for that. Lorelei still had the mindset of a teen. Probably got up at noon, made a few bracelets, and texted her friends. Easy life. But reality was coming.

They turned the corner to the library. This building, at least, had all the lights on. Micah held the door open for Lorelei and they stepped inside.

The air conditioning washed over them like a cool breeze.

The librarian looked up from her desk. "Why

hello, Micah," she said. She nodded at Lorelei. "Can I help you find something?"

"Hello, Cynthia. Lorelei and I plan to use a study room if there's one open," he said.

"There aren't many people about," Cynthia said. "I'm sure you can find something. But if you need me to let you into the historical books vault to use the table in there for privacy, just let me know."

"Will do," he said.

They walked past the magazine and newspaper racks. Between the stacks of nonfiction were doors to the private study rooms.

The first one was open, so they settled in opposite chairs, and Micah held out his hand for the packet Lorelei had been served.

She slid it over, and he glanced through the pages. "All standard stuff. It does say which part of the Civil Code you violated."

"I don't know what any of that means," Lorelei said.

"Well, fires are a special kind of crime. Although, murder can be, too."

When her eyes got wide, he waved his hands as if to brush away that thought. "Sorry, the lawyer in me is talking. What I mean is that there are both criminal and civil sides to some crimes. Arson, for example, is a crime you can be charged with and sent to jail."

When Lorelei started to sink in her chair, he

quickly added, "That's not what is happening to you. Judge Hughes wants this to be a civil matter."

"Okay," Lorelei said. "So is someone suing me?"

"Not exactly," Micah said. "As far as I can tell, this is basically the City of Applebottom versus you."

She sunk down in her chair or a little more. "Should I just move away? Not that I can afford it. But should I?"

"You can't move away from this problem. And really, I think the judge is just trying to help set you straight. He didn't want you to get off easy and think that it was no big deal that you'd caused a fire."

"Okay," Lorelei said. She sat back up in her chair. "So what we need to do?"

"I just need to know everything there is to know about what happened. The value of the items you threw out. Simple things."

They chatted for a while about what she'd tossed out and how long she'd lived with Linda. He noted that she didn't have renter's insurance, and that there was no history of any criminal activity on her record.

After another half hour, he folded up the piece of paper with his notes and tucked the pages back in the envelope.

"I think that about does it for now," he said. "The hearing is in a couple weeks. I'll put together some things and if I have more questions, I'll let you know."

Lorelei stood up. "Thank you so much, Micah. I don't know what I would be doing without you."

"That's what I'm here for," he said.

They walked through the quiet library. As they passed the front desk, Cynthia popped out of the small office behind it.

"How did it go?" she asked.

Micah felt her keen eyes taking him in, then assessing Lorelei. What was that about? "All good. Thank you."

"You two could come back here tomorrow! I'll reserve a space!"

"Thanks," Micah said. "We'll keep that in mind."

Cynthia waved at them in an overly friendly matter.

As soon as they cleared the door, Lorelei asked, "What was she so excited about?"

"No clue," Micah said. But his gut told him that between the conversation with Judge Hughes and the way Cynthia had acted, something unusual was afoot in Applebottom.

CHAPTER 7

*L*orelei was still in her pajamas on Saturday morning, working on bracelet number ten of the big order, when she got the call from Grandma Betty.

Lorelei really wished she could convert her grandmother to texting.

"What's up, Grandma?"

"I've got too many people down at the tea shop for me to handle," her grandmother said. "And Sandy is gone to New York for the week. I really need your help down here."

"But Grandma, I have all these bracelets to make!"

"It's just for a couple hours. It'll settle down by afternoon. It always does."

Lorelei sighed. The bracelets would get done. "Okay. I'll be up there in a few minutes."

"Why don't you wear that yellow sundress? It always looks so pretty on you."

Wait, what?

"I don't think I want to try making sandwiches in that, Grandma. But thank you."

"All right, sweetheart. But dress nice."

Lorelei ended the call, shaking her head. Yellow sundress? Dress nice? What was that all about?

She pinched the end of the bracelet so the beads wouldn't roll away, and headed to her closet. She touched the yellow sundress briefly before grabbing a pair of shorts and a pink T-shirt. It was just the tea shop. Grandma Betty didn't dress any fancier than usual when she worked there. She was known for her sparkly sweatsuits that matched her little poodle Clementine's ear bows.

She ran a quick brush through her hair and tied it up in a ponytail. She almost left, but at the last minute went back into the bathroom, added a quick swipe of eyeliner and some mascara, and rushed out.

Even though the walk was a short ten minutes, Lorelei wished she had taken her car. The sun overhead was merciless, and she was dripping with sweat by the time she made it to Tea for Two.

But when she pushed open the front door to the shop, everything became suddenly clear.

In the back corner, several tables were pushed together beneath a sign that read *Estate Planning for Seniors*. That explained the need for help. Seated there were some of Applebottom's older citizens, including Gertrude and Maude, the owners of the pie shop a few doors down. And Archie, the man who had been announcing the football games for decades.

In the center of them all, leading the discussion, was none other than Micah Livingston.

So that was why Grandma Betty had suggested the sundress.

Lorelei quickly swiped a finger beneath both eyes, hoping the sweat hadn't made her mascara run. She hustled along the counter and ducked beneath the open section that allowed her behind the sandwich case. Her grandmother was nowhere in sight.

As she hurried to the door to the back of the shop, Micah met her eye and gave her a brief nod.

Lorelei touched her hands to her sweaty forehead and smoothed some stray wisps that had fallen out of her ponytail. She was going to find her grandmother, and she was going to ask her what the heck was going on.

Micah worked hard to maintain a stoic courtroom expression as Lorelei rushed through the tea shop and hurried out of sight.

They had only passed a fleeting glance, but the urge to grin at her harried, sweaty walk was strong.

He tried to focus on Archie's lengthy explanation

about why he was there to plan his estate, but he couldn't quite get the image of Lorelei out of his mind.

Gertrude let out a grunt, her forehead wrinkling to the line of her fluffy white hair. "For Pete's sake, Archie, are you through yet?"

Micah snapped back to attention. Gertrude's patience had worn out. Not that there was much to begin with.

Gertrude fiddled with the neckline of her shiny black shirt, which she'd probably chosen to amplify the grimness of the occasion, and said, "You know good and well that your stock lives to be ninety-five. So quit your bellyaching about your colonoscopy, and let the rest of us have a chance to figure out what we're going to do when we pop off."

Micah struggled extra hard to maintain a straight expression after that little outburst. "So what brings you here, Gertrude?" he asked.

"I'm dying, of course!" Gertrude cried. "You think I'm gonna waste my Saturday if I'm not?"

"I'm sorry," Micah said. "I hadn't heard."

In the chair next to Gertrude, Maude shook her head, making the gray bits in her tight black curls sparkle in the light. "That's because it isn't true," she said. "Gertrude here found out her blood pressure was a little high, and now she's sure she's going to have a stroke any minute."

"Don't make fun of the dying," Gertrude snapped.

"Gertie, you're making a mountain out of a mole-hill. You're just mad that Doc Stevens told you to reduce your salt."

"Maude Lewis, you and I have owned this pie shop together for thirty years, and you know exactly what I eat every day. How am I going to get a decent piece of pork in this town without any salt?"

"I think if you eat it the way it's served it will be fine," Maude shot back. "Just don't empty the shaker on it."

Micah slid his hands forward on the table to get their attention. "Ladies," he said. "Health concerns are a very important reason to think about your estate planning. Now, I do agree with Maude that we are not in any sort of crisis situation. Let's stay focused on the task at hand."

Gertrude sat back in her chair. "You guys will be sorry when I'm dead by Tuesday."

Micah sighed. Gertrude had always been a little dramatic. "Gertrude, as I understand it, you have no family to leave your half of the pie shop to, correct?"

"That's right," Gertrude said. "Parents, long gone." She looked pleased, as if this proved her point that she would die any second. "No husband. No kids." She glanced over at Maude. "And stuck with her as my business partner."

Maude patted her arm. "I love you too, honey." She turned to Micah. "I have spoken about this with my kids, and if I should die before Gertrude, I prefer to have my half of the pie shop be left to her."

Micah jotted this down. "Good, good. We can draw that up. How is the pie shop organized as a business? Limited liability company? Did you incorporate? Is it still a sole proprietorship?"

"You're speaking Greek to me," Gertrude said.

"It's a rather informal arrangement," Maude said.

"It might be good idea to tighten that up," Micah said. "That's a little bit more than we can handle in this workshop, but you can give me a call and we can go over all that."

"That would be just fine," Maude said.

Rather than try to tackle Gertrude again, Micah turned back to Archie. "Do you have a lot of assets that you need to organize?" he asked.

As Archie went on another long spiel about his classic cars in various stages of disrepair, Micah noticed Lorelei had returned to stand behind the counter.

She'd taken her hair down, and it was brushed and fluffy. Her lips were surprisingly pink, which he hadn't noticed earlier. Perhaps she had put on a little lipstick.

Was that for *him*? Or more likely, Betty had insisted she look a certain way to serve customers.

He bet Lorelei didn't like being told how to look.

She was definitely put out, her arms crossed over a pink Tea for Two apron. Their eyes met, and she relaxed a little, giving him a half-smile. He gave her another nod and shifted his gaze back to Archie.

When the workshop finally came to an end, Micah stood and shook all their hands. "Let me know if I can help you more," he said. "Take these worksheets home and fill them out."

"I told you he'd get us in so he could charge us big money," Gertrude said stonily.

"Actually," Micah said," if you bring these back to the next workshop, we can get your will handled right here. It's only if we need to actually file some legal documents that incur county or state fees that we start looking at exchanging money."

Gertrude gave a little *harrumph* but picked up one of the sheets. Archie took his. Maude leaned forward to kiss Micah on the cheek. "Thank you, love. Gertrude's just a little put out about her health at the moment. It will be all right."

"You take care of her," Micah said.

"You know I will."

Micah gathered his papers and folders as the others filed out. He realized that Betty had disappeared completely since Lorelei showed up. After a moment, they were the only two left in the shop.

"Betty pressed you into service?" he asked.

"Said she needed some help," Lorelei said. "I've made exactly two cups of tea the entire time I've been here."

"She busy in the back?"

"It's taken her an hour to make pimento cheese sandwiches," Lorelei said. "I smell a rat."

Micah moved the tables back to their former positions and fixed all the chairs. Then he headed up to the counter. "I don't guess I could convince you to snag me one of those sandwiches and some iced tea?"

"Sure. Regular or hibiscus?"

"Hibiscus."

"I assume you want sweet, otherwise you get run out of town."

"Of course. Can't have the lynch mob after me."

She scooped ice into a glass and filled it with tea.

"Let me go check on the sandwiches," she said, sliding the glass across the counter. "I'll be right back."

Betty breezed in from the back room, carrying a tray. "Got them right here."

Lorelei paused, her hand on her hip. "You been listening the whole time?"

"I have no idea what you're talking about!" Betty's glittery track suit sparkled as she opened the case and shoved the tray inside. Then she was gone again.

"That's pretty suspicious," Lorelei said.

"They mean well," Micah said. "They know I'm helping you out."

Lorelei reopened the case and placed a sandwich on a shiny white porcelain plate. "Apple chips or potato crisps with that?"

"Potato." He glanced around. "Do you think she

would object to you sitting with me? Having some tea?"

Betty rushed back out into the main store. "I'm all good, Lorelei," she said. She reached behind Lorelei to untie the apron. "Thank you for your help. What kind of tea would you like, sweetheart?"

"I can get it," Lorelei said, shrugging off the apron.

"Oh, no. Let me." Betty picked up the plate and passed it to Micah. "No charge for this," she said. "Thanks for bringing people into the shop today."

"Thank you for providing space," he said. He picked up his tea and plate. "Meet you in the corner?"

She nodded.

He headed to the back to wait.

Funny how this worked out. Him and Lorelei, having another opportunity to meet.

This town was up to something.

CHAPTER 8

*L*orelei didn't miss the sly grin on her grandmother's face as she passed by with her glass of tea to join Micah in the back corner of the shop.

There was no doubt in her mind that her grandmother had called her to help her today for the sole reason that Micah was here. But to what end? Micah was six or seven years older than her, stable, mature, a lawyer, a pillar of the community.

She was the town screwup who set the yard on fire.

What were they hoping for?

She slid into a chair next to Micah. "So how did it go with the estate planning?"

"Gertrude is sure she's gonna have a stroke any day," Micah said. "Archie provided me way too many details about his colon."

Lorelei laughed. "I was trying not to listen in."

"Me too," Micah said. "Then I remembered that I was in charge."

He took a bite of the sandwich, and Lorelei found herself admiring his strong, elegant hands. She spotted Grandma Betty hovering by the cash register, watching them intently, and forced herself to look away.

"Was there anything new you needed from me about my hearing?" Lorelei asked. "I tried reading it all again, but I swear it's written in an alien language."

"I'll review everything next week," he said. "It should be pretty straightforward."

"So, what could happen?" she asked. "Are they going to fine me or something? Can you go to jail on a civil case?"

"No, there won't be jail time. Technically there could be a fine. But most likely you'll be given some sort of community service."

"That's okay I guess," she said.

"Been doing any paper shaking lately?" His voice got so low and rumbly that Lorelei felt it all the way to her knees.

Lorelei glanced over at her grandmother, who quickly shifted her gaze away, and lowered her tone as well. "Do you like a girl in hair rollers?"

He laughed, and this one went all the way to her toes.

The tables at Tea for Two were small, so they

were sitting as close as they had ever been. Lorelei caught a whiff of something woodsy, aftershave perhaps. Micah wasn't wearing a full suit, but he did have on a button-down shirt and tie. She guessed he had to look lawyerly as he ran his estate planning.

"Why do you do these workshops?" she asked.

He swallowed his bite. "It's helpful to people. It reminds them to think about these things, whether they need my actual services or not."

"So it's part of your do-gooder nature? Like being a volunteer firefighter?"

"I don't think of it as being a do-gooder. Just being part of the community."

"I don't think your dad did that, did he?" Lorelei asked.

Micah shook his head. "No. Not that I know of. But then he had a family and lots of other things to do."

Lorelei sat back in her chair. It hadn't occurred to her that maybe Micah was bored in Applebottom. He'd said this wasn't where he intended to land, that he wanted a big city. She wondered if he would eventually leave.

"Is your dad completely retired? Are you going to be running his practice forever?"

Micah folded his paper napkin and set it on top of his uneaten crust. He was like her, willing to eat the sides and bottom, but not the rounded top. Sandwich twins.

"I'm not really sure I know the answer to that. I get the feeling that he'll eventually get tired of traveling and want to settle back in with some cases."

"What would he have done if you had refused?"

"I don't think that was an option," Micah said.

A movement behind the counter caught Lorelei's eye. Grandma Betty was edging closer and closer to them, trying to listen in on their conversation.

Good grief. She leaned close to him. "You want to go somewhere?"

His eyebrows lifted with surprise. "You mean now?"

"Yeah," she said. "Get away from my meddling grandmother." She said the last two words in a whisper.

His head bent near hers, and her heart fluttered faster. What was that all about? She felt like a sixteen-year-old. This was Micah Livingston, the town lawyer. What was her heart thinking, tip-tapping like it was?

Nevertheless, it was happening, and she didn't want this conversation to end. Nor did she want her grandmotherly chaperone. They had to get out of here.

"How about we head to the park? I could meet you in front of your law office in five minutes."

His eyes met hers for a moment, and she realized that she had just taken a really big chance. Micah might not want to talk to her more. Maybe he really was just being nice to help her with the case.

Maybe he was already dating someone. Sometime elegant. Poised. Smart.

Someone who didn't set things on fire.

But as their gazes lingered, she realized no, she was right. He wanted to keep talking to her, too.

"A secret meeting," he said. "I'm in. See you in five."

She stood up and picked up both of their glasses and his plate.

"Thank you for helping out Applebottom's finest citizens," she said loud enough for Grandma Betty to hear. "Talk to you soon about the court date."

Micah picked up his leather briefcase and pushed in his chair. "Absolutely." He turned to the counter. "Thank you, Betty, for the tea and sandwich."

"Anytime!" Grandma Betty called.

Lorelei took the plate and glasses to the busing station.

"See you later, Grandma. Glad I could help. Gotta go make those bracelets."

Grandma Betty had picked up her poodle Clementine and idly stroked her as she watched Lorelei duck beneath the counter to grab her purse.

"You two sure didn't talk for long," she said.

"We said everything that needed to be said. I think we have one more meeting before the hearing, though. See you later!"

She whirled around and hustled out of the shop. Now maybe she could have a conversation with Micah without the watchful eyes of her kin, and figure out this sputtering feeling in her belly.

❧

Micah quickly surveyed the contents of the small wardrobe in the back of his office. It was a hot day, and he was wearing completely inappropriate clothes for a walk to the park.

After a moment, he decided to go all the way casual, pulling out a pair of running shorts and a T-shirt. He didn't really have anything in between, not at the office.

He changed swiftly and left his folded business clothes at the bottom of the cabinet.

Interesting that Lorelei had asked him on an outing. He was willing to go with it. Something about her stuck in his mind. As much as he liked to discount her as young and frivolous, he was captivated. She had a spunk and fire that maybe he had been missing.

When he passed his secretary's desk, he immediately spotted Lorelei sitting on the bench outside. Her back was to the plate glass windows, and she was simply watching the cars go by.

She hadn't wanted her grandmother to know they were meeting. Not that their activities could be hidden in Applebottom. If the two of them were going to walk to the park, they would be seen within a block, and by the time they actually arrived at the hillside overlooking the lake, two thirds of Applebottom would already be buzzing about their little jaunt.

He wondered if Lorelei had thought this through.

Perhaps it didn't matter.

He opened the door and gave her a little wave.

She stood up. "Why Micah Livingston, you actually have legs."

He laughed as he turned to lock the door. "I can wear shorts like the rest of you peasants."

"That's funny," she said. "Because I really do feel like a peasant."

"Are you kidding? Your grandmother is one of the Town Square proprietors. That's practically royalty around here."

"I don't know. You seem pretty King of the Hill."

"Nonsense. Shall we cut through the gazebo or circle the square to slow down the gossip?"

"Back streets," Lorelei said. "Although I have a feeling we've been set up, possibly more than once."

Micah considered this. "Well, they didn't start the fire."

Lorelei's face colored pink. "No, but Grandma Betty definitely called me for help that she didn't need this morning because you were there."

"You think they're up to their old tricks again?"

"Who?"

"Your grandmother and the others. You do know they're the ones who pushed Sandy and Andrew together."

"Really? I thought they'd been together like, forever."

"No. It was Betty's doing. And the football coach — Carter McBride. He helped Ginny with her dog, because Delilah made him."

"Huh. That must have been before I moved back."

"They might be going full matchmaker."

Lorelei cut her eyes at him. "You mean the two of us?"

"I've suspected something. I had no clue why Judge Hughes would handle your case like this." Micah led them down a back street, careful to avoid walking by his own house. That might lead to a little *too* much gossip.

"So what do we do about it?" Lorelei asked.

"I don't know. I guess until the hearing is over, they're going to throw us together."

"Good grief," Lorelei said. "Those crazy ladies."

"One of them is your grandmother."

"Don't I know it."

They walked along in silence for a while. A cluster of kids ran through sprinklers on a lawn near the end of the street.

"Cute," Lorelei said. "I guess I'll have a nephew soon."

"When is Mandy due?"

"November."

"You like kids?"

"Sure. Not part of my immediate plans, but maybe down the line." She cut her eyes at him again. "What about you?"

"I'm the only child these days, so I'll be expected to deliver." He laughed. "One of the good things about Mom living on cruise ships is that she isn't around to pester me about my love life."

They turned toward the walking path that led to the park. Several joggers puttered along the path, sweating profusely.

"My parents don't seem to have many expectations from me right now," Lorelei said. "Mandy has them fully occupied with her perfect domesticity."

"That's the nice thing about having a sibling. You always have a buffer between yourself and your parents."

"Has it been hard? Since Josh, I mean."

Micah kept his gaze on the path. The air was still, the sun directly overhead. Even the shadows were scant.

"It gets easier over time," he said. "When I first came back, that was the worst. While I was away, it was easier to imagine he was still home, kicking back on the sofa watching the Razorbacks. He went to U of A too, you know."

"I did," she said. "I was a freshman when he gradu-ated. I guess he enlisted right after that?"

"Yeah, it was the only thing he could think of that Dad wouldn't question if he didn't go into law. Dad has a lot of respect for military. He was pretty proud."

"I bet."

"I still see him places," Micah said. They were approaching the hill. He pointed into the woods to their left. "Back through there is the clearing where there used to be one of the original houses."

"Right. The old Hempstead Place."

"Exactly. Josh and I used to go there and shoot BB guns."

"Oh, Officer Tatum would have nailed you on that if you got caught."

"We knew it. I miss that old man."

"You might be alone in that." Lorelei laughed. "He was one sourpuss."

"The male version of Gertrude?" Micah said, and they laughed again. "Who knows. I might be just as crotchety in my old age."

"Heaven help us," Lorelei said.

They climbed the hill, and the lake spread out in front of them, sparkling and white-blue.

"Sure is pretty," Lorelei said, "even though it's hot."

"It is."

They passed the playground, where a few swel-tering parents pushed their kids on swings.

Lorelei pointed toward the dock. "Want to get your feet wet?"

"Sure," Micah said. He knew where she wanted to go. That was the nice thing about being with someone who grew up in the same town as you. There were little haunts that would be familiar to you both.

"Mandy and I used to come down here and eat popsicles," Lorelei said. "They would always be half-melted by the time we scrambled down the rocks, but somehow they just tasted better with your feet dunked in the lake."

"I know exactly what you mean," Micah said.

They left the path and picked their way through the rocks. Farther along the shore, closer to the mayor's RV Park, sand had been hauled in to form a little beach. But along the public park, you had to stumble down the jagged slope to get to the water.

They moved slowly and carefully, until they passed beneath the dock. The shade was merciful and cool.

"So much better," Lorelei said.

"Now if we only had popsicles," Micah said.

Lorelei slipped on a loose rock, and before she could right herself, Micah's hand shot out and grasped hers.

"You okay?" he asked.

"Grace and poise were never my strong suit," she said.

She shot him a quick smile as their grips fumbled, but they held onto each other as they continued beneath the dock.

They reached the end. "I can't believe this concrete slab is still here," Lorelei said.

"Somebody told me it was poured specifically to give us a place to sit. Some generation before ours." Micah released her hand, and the two of them sat on the rough, flat surface of the concrete. It angled down and provided just the right amount of overlap so that you could dangle your legs off the edge and get your feet wet.

"Well, huzzah to the previous generation for knowing what to do." Lorelei kicked off her sandals and dipped her toes in the water. "This is about the most perfect thing to do on a day like this."

Micah untied his shoes. "It certainly beats working."

Lorelei leaned back on her arms, kicking her feet so that water sprayed out into the lake. "Is that what you do on Saturdays? Work more?"

Micah set his shoes behind him and tucked the socks inside. "Sometimes. I try not to, though."

The water felt heavenly. He scooted forward on the concrete, sinking into the water to his calves.

Lorelei legs were evenly tan, and long, just as he remembered from seeing them in the pink getup the other night. He had to force his eyes away.

"What do you do on weekends?" he asked.

"Sometimes I hang out with my friends. During the summer, though, Candace is off, since she's a teacher, so one day sort of blends into the other. Sometimes I help Grandma Betty, like today. When she's actually busy."

"Sounds like a nice life," Micah said. He laced his fingers together behind his head and leaned back on the warm concrete. It felt mighty fine in the shade. He closed his eyes. The shouts of the children from the playground behind them echoed under the dock, along with little splashes as Lorelei kicked her feet. Off in the woods, birds called and twittered about. Here and there, a few dogs barked.

Yes, this was a fine Saturday.

The splashing stopped and he peered over at Lorelei. She had laid back, too, her eyes closed.

Micah couldn't remember having a moment like this with a woman. Sure, as a kid, he and his friends would chill out on the dock, but dating had always been contentious. Girls were a lot of maintenance, needing attention. They clung to his arm, or tried to steer his attention.

Not that he minded. It was just different from this.

The warmth. The quiet. The peace.

It was easy.

CHAPTER 9

*L*orelei had just packaged up the first half of her big bracelet order when a strange envelope slid under her door.

Linda, no doubt. That woman was strange. She often shoved mail into Lorelei's room that way. Lorelei had developed the habit of looking down when she opened her door, to make sure she didn't step on it.

But this was midday on a Wednesday. The mail wouldn't come for hours, and she already had yesterday's batch.

Lorelei arranged the pretty silk baggies in the box and got up to stretch. She was at a stopping point anyway. Forty bracelets down and forty to go.

Turns out these were for a sweet sixteen party. Must be an epic one, with eighty guests. Lorelei's own sweet sixteen had been a simple affair, a beach party down at the RV Park. Ten friends or so, swimming, barbecue, and a sound system T-bone had set up just for her to have music.

It was a good memory.

Lorelei walked over to the door and snatched up the envelope. It didn't have postage on it, or an address. Scrawled on the front, in Linda's chicken-scratch handwriting, were the words *sign and return.*

Lorelei's heart pounded. Was this something to do with the court hearing? It was still over a week away. Micah hadn't told her she needed to do anything else.

She pulled out a sheaf of pages and read the top.

Residential Lease Agreement.

Great. Now Linda wanted a contract. Right as Lorelei was running out of money and wasn't sure she could stay.

Lorelei quickly scanned the document. She had lived in the dorm in college, so she'd never seen a lease agreement. She didn't know what was normal. She paused on *security deposit.* So now Linda wanted a hundred bucks from her in case she ruined something.

There was an entire section about liability for damages. Linda had highlighted it in yellow.

Term of lease. Minimum six months. Six months! Lorelei had no idea where she would be in six months. That would be past Christmas!

She couldn't sign this. She wondered what would happen if she didn't. Was this Linda's way of pushing her out? The woman couldn't even say it to her face?

Her first temptation was to call her dad. Or her mom. Or even Grandma Betty, who was in the quilting circle with Linda and would tell her to back off.

But then, she thought, why not ask Micah? He was her lawyer. This seemed related to her case, and he would understand the lease.

Yes. She would go see him.

This time Lorelei really did put on the yellow sundress, a pair of pretty white sandals, and straightened her hair.

Probably people would notice that she had dolled up, but she didn't care. Weren't you supposed to dress nicely when you visited a law office?

She also took her car this time, so she wouldn't be a sweaty mess by the time she got there. Lorelei sent a little apology up to the environment as she parked her car along the side streets near Micah's law office.

Why was she nervous? This was official business. Only as she reached the front door and placed her hand on the handle did she realize, what if he wasn't here? Maybe she should've called ahead.

She let go of the handle. Was it rude to just show up at a lawyer's office and ask to see him?

Her courage faltered.

Unfortunately, she stood in front of a large pane of glass that made her perfectly visible to Marianne, the middle-aged secretary who worked for Micah. Marianne had already seen her and was waving her inside.

Too late. Worst case scenario, she could just leave the lease for Micah to look over.

The inside of the office was cool, the air conditioning caressing her skin.

"Why hello, Lorelei," Marianne said pleasantly. She wore a pink sweater over her dress, a testament to the temperature inside the office. "Can I help you?"

"Is Micah here?" Lorelei faltered. "I mean, I don't have to see him, I can drop this off, but I got a thing from my landlord, and it seemed sort of related to what happened." She didn't want to say anything about the fire out loud. Marianne surely knew, but that didn't mean Lorelei had to bring it up.

"He's here, but he might still be on a conference call," Marianne said. Her eyes darted to the phone on her desk.

"Okay."

None of the lights on the phone were lit up. That should have meant that Micah wasn't on the line, but maybe he preferred Marianne to keep any distractions away while he was working. Lorelei wanted to curl up into a little ball and roll herself out the door. She had been stupidly presumptuous in coming there. Just because she and Micah had walked to the lake didn't mean that he was going to put off all his regular clients for this free work he was doing as a favor.

But just as she slid the envelope onto Marianne's desk to leave for Micah, his head popped past the frame of the door to the back office. "Lorelei? Is everything okay?"

A stupidly huge smile took over her face, and nothing she could do seemed to be able to calm it down. "You're here! I mean, of course you're here. Marianne said you were here. But you're not on the phone!"

Lord, she sounded like a ten-year-old with a crush.

She snatched up the envelope. "I can't tell if Linda's trying to kick me out of my place," she said quickly. "She sent me a lease. We didn't have one before. It seems like maybe her intention is to get me out. Can you read it?"

Micah stepped out of his office, his tie loose at his collar and the top button of his crisp white shirt left open. Otherwise, he was immaculately dressed in charcoal suit pants and perfectly polished shoes. Her heart caught a little.

"Come back here," he said. "Let's take a look at it."

The office smelled of wood polish. She tried to take it all in with a glance, so she didn't seem nosy. Tall shelves were lined with leather books. His polished mahogany desk had a glass top and a sleek computer on one corner. An antique wardrobe filled a back wall.

She loved it. It was so classic and masculine. To one side was a small leather sofa and a matching chair.

Wow. Micah really knew how to *adult*. Everything was so professional. It almost didn't fit the man she'd sat with under the dock.

Micah sat in the chair and gestured to the small sofa. "Let's sit over here. I can review this real quick to see if I can spot Linda's intention. It looks like a generic lease. Did you talk to her about it?"

"No. She slid it under my door. That's what has me worried. Plus she highlighted the part about liability."

"I see that."

He flipped through the pages, his eyes scanning the lines.

Lorelei continued to look around, spying the map of the world that was handsomely framed over his head. Both his law degree and his father's were up on the wall as well.

His world was almost precisely the opposite of hers, all mismatched pillows and sentimental trinkets. He dealt with real world problems, while she fussed over which color beads to accent a bit of dyed leather.

So why was her heart hammering so hard?

The lease, of course. The prospect of having to move back in with her parents.

A zillion plans zipped through her mind, discarded as impractical. She'd messed up, bad. She needed to finish her degree. Get a real job. Be more like Micah.

He seemed so solid. So sure of himself. That was all this was. He represented security. Knowing what you were doing each day. And he could be spontaneous. He'd gone to the dock.

It wasn't like he was straitlaced. She remembered his reputation for parties.

Maybe at his heart, he was like her.

Maybe with his influence, she could be more like him.

His head popped up. "I really don't think she's trying to pull one over on you, Lorelei," he said. "It's just a lease she downloaded off the Internet. She's asking for a deposit and a six-month commitment from you, though. And all this is standard so that if you damage something, she can be compensated."

Lorelei's hands fluttered in her lap. "Okay. Thank you. Sorry. I panicked."

He passed the lease back to her. "There's no need. You going to sign it? You have thirty days to decide and then you have to move out."

"Really? Shoot. I'm not sure I can commit to that."

He sat back in his chair. "You planning to move?"

"No, I just…" She didn't really want to admit that she might not be able to pay rent. "I'm just not sure where I'll be for that long. I should probably find a job."

"Surely there's something around Applebottom. Maybe up at one of the schools? You could definitely substitute with the amount of college hours you have."

"Oh, gosh, no! I couldn't do that. I don't have the patience."

Micah tried to hold back his grin, but she spotted it.

"Don't laugh! I'd like to see you handle spit wads and switching seats and all the little tricks they do to subs. Don't tell me you were an angel when Mrs. Winchell used to come."

He gave in and laughed. "I'd forgotten all about poor Mrs. Winchell. Is she still doing it?"

"As far as I know. But I don't think I'm up for it."

Micah leaned forward, bracing his hands on his knees. Her throat constricted. Those hands. There they were again.

"I think T-bone was looking for some help at the RV Park. Seems like he's had an uptick in people coming and he wants someone to check them in so he can still roam about."

"You think I'd be good at that?" she asked. "T-bone scares me."

Micah chuckled. "T-bone scares everybody."

"I guess he's the reason why there's never any trouble at the RV Park."

"Oh, there's trouble. Sometimes I see them at court."

"But you don't represent them?"

"I do civil cases, not criminal. But it's a small court. I see the docket."

"Docket?"

"The list of cases being heard by the judge."

Lorelei fussed with the packet in her lap, fiddling the corners. This was all very much outside her world.

"You think you can coast on your jewelry making business?" he asked.

"You know about that?"

"They were all out on your desk. You have an online store?"

"I do. I just need to scale up. I haven't figured that piece out."

He stared at the ceiling for a moment, tapping his knee. "I swear I read something really good about that recently. How to maximize searches, finding the right niche."

"You read something like that?"

"It's the same for law firms. You don't want a million pointless inquiries taking up your time. You want the right clicks."

"Oh! Yes. That makes sense."

"I'll forward it on if I see it." He stood up. "It's

lunch time. Or close enough. You want to walk down to Betty's?"

Had he just asked her to lunch?

"Can I say yes to lunch and no to having my grandmother eavesdrop?"

"Point taken. Annabelle's? I'm afraid I don't have time for a trip to Branson midday."

"Annabelle's is fine. If we sit next to the jukebox and play some heavy metal, no one will be able to listen to us."

"Sounds like a definite plan." He held out his hand to help her up.

She hesitated a moment, then took it. His hand was warm on her chilly one. After she stood, he held it a few seconds longer than necessary, then released her and began to button his shirt and tighten his tie.

The motion felt familiar, like she was his wife, watching him dress in the morning. She swallowed hard. That was a crazy idea. Who would think in a million years that the college dropout would imagine such a thing with the town lawyer?

But as they headed out in the sunshiny summer day to have lunch together at the local diner, she realized something important.

She hadn't even thought about Gary in days.

CHAPTER 10

Micah had barely sat down at his desk again after a most enjoyable, laugh-filled lunch with Lorelei when Marianne buzzed him on his phone.

"Judge Hughes is on the line," she said. "He sounds gruffer than usual."

Interesting. Micah punched the button to pick up the call.

"This is Micah Livingston."

"Micah, my son, it has been brought to my attention that you had lunch with Miss Lorelei Spencer today."

That was fast. Of course, they had gone to Annabelle's Café, where half the town would see them, but it wasn't like he expected someone to report to the judge.

"We did. Lorelei came by to bring me a new document given to her by her landlord and was concerned that she was being pushed out of her home due to the incident. It was absolutely a matter related to her hearing."

"Hogwash," the judge said. "You were making googly eyes at each other."

"Sir, I—"

"Hush and listen. I know that quite a few of the ladies in this town would like to see the two of you together, but when I agreed to have you take on her case, I never had any idea that a young lawyer with such good standing in our community would fraternize with a client while still under attorney-client privilege. This is abuse of your power dynamic, and you could be reported to the bar."

Micah sat back in his chair. "Judge Hughes, I can assure you, there is nothing going on between me and Lorelei. It was a simple lunch."

"Just four days after the two of you were seen holding hands beneath the dock at Applebottom Park."

"She'd slipped on the rocks."

"And you were there *with her* on the rocks," the judge bellowed. "This girl is seven years your junior. She's in a tumultuous time in her life. This is no time to be taking advantage of her affections."

Micah forced himself to stay calm. "I absolutely agree that it was inappropriate for me to have gone to the park with Lorelei while we were still working on this case. But I assure you there is no relationship between us."

"There better not be," the judge said. "But since I have these women breathing down my neck on one side, and the two of you practically getting hitched on the other side, I have no choice but to make a change to our hearing."

Micah couldn't believe this. He and Lorelei hadn't even *kissed*. Not even *close*. "Are you taking me off the case?"

"No. I've moved you up to tomorrow. And don't go out with her tonight. Don't you go anywhere near that girl until our hearing is done and you are no longer her attorney. Do you hear me?"

"Loud and clear," Micah said.

The line went dead. Micah loosened his tie and unbuttoned his shirt collar again. Well, that was something. It hadn't even occurred to him to think about the whole attorney-client privilege thing. He didn't handle cases like this normally. He was just helping her out as a favor to the judge. The same judge who'd just read him the riot act.

But it was true. He knew better. The moment that he'd seen her in her bedroom in her little 1950s nightie, he should've known to back far, far away.

The truth was on his side. But this was a small town, and propriety came first.

He would set this straight. He buzzed his phone. "Marianne?"

"Yes, Micah."

"The judge just moved Lorelei Spencer's hearing up to tomorrow. Can you call Lorelei to let her know about the change? And if you can somehow tactfully suggest that she dress conservatively, I would appreciate it."

For a moment, there was an empty pause. He practically dared her to say anything about his lunch.

Finally, she said, "Will do."

"Thank you."

He loosened his tie another inch. This whole thing was too much. He set aside some paperwork for a case he'd be handling next week and pulled forward the information for Lorelei's case tomorrow. He'd have to rearrange his schedule a little bit, but that was easy enough to do. If the judge wanted her case cleared by tomorrow, they would get it cleared.

And of course, that meant as of tomorrow afternoon, he would no longer be her attorney.

CHAPTER 11

*L*orelei wasn't sure why she thought she would be able to get away with going to the hearing without her family getting involved.

This *was* Applebottom, after all.

When she went downstairs wearing the most conservative thing in her wardrobe, a black skirt with a short-sleeved white sweater, her mother stood by the door, speaking with Linda.

The two women looked up as Lorelei slowed her steps.

Great. Just great.

Her mother looked her up and down. "You march yourself right upstairs, young lady, and put on that dark blue suit I bought you two years ago to wear to Great Aunt Ethel's funeral.

"Mom, it's ninety degrees outside. That one is long sleeved and wool. I will die of heat stroke."

"I don't want to hear one more word from you. Marianne already called me to make sure you were dressed proper for court, and I'm telling you to go upstairs and change."

Linda stood tall and straight-backed, a self-satisfied smile on her face. Lorelei closed her eyes for a minute and pressed her fingernails into her palms. She was twenty-four years old. This could not be happening.

"Time is wasting, young lady," her mother said. "Now go."

It was easier just to change her clothes. If she collapsed from heat exhaustion, her mother could feel bad later.

When she returned, her mother and Linda had been joined by Grandma Betty, Lorelei's other grandma Etta Humphries, Uncle Sam, and her mother's best friend Doris McCallister from the quilting circle.

"It's just a little hearing," Lorelei cried. "You guys are acting like I'm about to go to jail."

Her mother straightened the waistline of her port-wine church dress. "I want to make sure Judge Hughes knows that my daughter has the full backing of her family, who will endeavor to set her straight from this day forward."

Linda nodded enthusiastically.

"Do we even have a car that will carry all of us?" Lorelei asked.

"I have your sister Mandy's new minivan," her mother said. "It holds seven, if I take out Shila's car seat."

"I was planning to take my own car," Lorelei said.

"That won't be necessary. Your father is going to drive. He's waiting in the car."

"Doesn't he have to go to work?"

"Not when his little girl is in trouble." Her mother opened the front door and started shooing people through it. "Come along now."

When they stepped out into the blistering sunshine, Lorelei briefly considered making a run for it. This was entirely too much to bear. Heaven help her if word ever got back to Gary about this fiasco that resulted from their breakup. She would never survive the mortification.

They all squeezed into the shiny white minivan that still smelled of new vinyl. Lorelei was sent all the way to the back with Uncle Sam and Doris. Her two grandmothers got the middle seats.

"How did you even know the hearing had been moved up?" Lorelei asked. She hadn't told anybody the original date, either.

Her mother glanced back from the front row. "You've forgotten that Judge Hughes's secretary June is Linda's sister-in-law."

Lorelei sat on the information for a minute. So Linda could have called her sister-in-law June, who let the judge know about the fire. It was probably her fault this whole thing was happening. They must have insisted the judge do something.

Lorelei still hadn't done anything with that lease. She'd figured that since the hearing had been moved up, she might as well wait and see what happened. For all she knew, they were going to run her out of town.

No. That would never happen. Her family had been in Applebottom too long. Grandma Betty was loved by everybody. Who knew what those people were thinking.

Maybe she didn't want to live in Linda's upstairs any longer anyway.

She leaned down to adjust the air conditioning, grateful that this new style of minivan had extra air vents in the back. She pointed one directly at her face.

The ride to the courthouse was mercifully short. The low building stood behind the tiny City Hall and police station. They parked on the corner and Lorelei peered across the square toward Micah's office building. The street was quiet, with only a lone lady walking into Janine's Spa.

Micah was probably already in the courtroom.

Lorelei waited for the others to get out, then squeezed between the seats. Now that they had arrived at the courthouse, her stomach had started to quiver a little. Maybe it wasn't such a bad thing to have family there, even if they were judging her more harshly than any of the officials inside the building.

"Stop your lollygagging," her mother chided her as they headed into the building.

Lorelei sighed. She couldn't do anything right. No doubt if she picked up her pace, her mother would complain that she was walking too fast

This was just as bad as when she showed up at home, her little car stuffed to the brim with everything that had once been in her dorm room, to confess that she had dropped out of school.

Maybe worse.

The guard checked them in and pointed the way to the courtroom. "They're still working on the morning docket," he said, "so you best be quiet as you go in."

Lorelei's entourage nodded solemnly and headed for the heavy wood door.

Inside the courtroom, Micah sat at the front table, which was spread with all manner of paper and folders. A man and a young woman that Lorelei didn't recognize sat opposite him.

The woman glanced back as they entered, and Lorelei felt a pang. She was really beautiful, with long copper hair and a smart dove-gray suit. As the woman turned back around, her eyes rested on Micah for a moment, and this time the emotion that zipped through Lorelei spiked hot. Did she know him? Had they dated? Was she another lawyer? The sort of girl that Micah ought to be dating?

Shush, Lorelei. It wasn't like Micah was dating Lorelei. They'd done nothing more than take a walk down to the park and have lunch.

But Lorelei felt like something might be there. The way he smiled at her. He never turned her down, she realized. Maybe she should do something impulsive and hair brained, as a test. Ask him on a real date.

Micah responded to whatever the other man had said. Her family scooted along the chairs, finally settling down with Lorelei at the end of the row.

Lorelei pressed her hand to her belly. This was a fine mess she'd gotten herself into. At least after today, it should be over. Both Micah and the other lawyer exchanged a few more words, then the judge banged his gavel and whatever they were doing seemed to be over. Micah stood and walked over to the other man, and they shook hands. The copper-haired girl stood as well, and extended her arm for a handshake.

Lorelei watched closely. Did they already know each other? Micah's smile for her seemed bigger than for the man. And the two of them definitely talked longer.

Lorelei felt her mother's eyes on her and realized she was gripping the edge of her chair. She forced herself to let loose and relax her shoulders.

The other lawyer and the woman quickly packed their things and walked up the aisle, passing directly beside Lorelei. The woman spotted Lorelei staring at her, and quickly Lorelei averted her eyes.

Man, she was pretty.

Lorelei had seen girls like that before, back when she was still in college. Smart, beautiful, self-assured. Lorelei wondered what it was like to go through life like that, knowing the world could be at your feet.

But then, her friend Candace was just as beautiful, and Lorelei knew for a fact that Candace felt like she was going nowhere. You never knew someone's problems unless you walked in their shoes.

She sure wished someone else would walk in her shoes right now.

Another man in a guard uniform stood at the end of the tall desk where Judge Hughes sat, and turned a piece of paper around so he could read it.

"Will the parties for case 742.3, the city of Applebottom vs. Lorelei Spencer, please step forward."

This was it. Micah stood up and turned, waving her toward him. Lorelei walked on unsteady legs to the front of the courtroom. Micah opened a little gate, and she passed through.

Micah gave her a quick smile. "Don't worry. Everything is fine. You'll sit over here by me."

"Do I have to swear on the Bible or something?" she whispered.

Another smile. "That's only if you're going to testify."

Micah had told her she probably would not have to do much of anything but be present. The lawyers would handle the talking.

A woman came forward and sat at the opposite table, opening a file.

Lorelei vaguely recognized her as someone she'd seen around town. She must work for the city or something.

Judge Hughes flipped through some papers, his expression stern. "Miss Spencer, I trust you have been made well aware of why you are here today?"

Micah had told her how to respond to this. "I have, your honor."

"Very well," he said. "Opening statements."

The other woman began speaking, listing off numbers and letters of code violations that Lorelei couldn't quite follow. She didn't see how anybody could ever represent themselves in something like this. She had no clue what was going on.

After what seemed like forever, the judge asked Micah for his statement. He was a little easier to follow, recounting the events of the fire and reviewing some of the documents that they had talked about, including her insurance and the value of the items.

"It's important to note that no actual property damage was sustained beyond what was intended to be discarded," Micah said. "There were no insurance losses, and no one was hurt."

The other woman spoke. "I would like to submit to the court the approximate cost of the average response by our volunteer fire department when it must answer a call. Remember to also factor in the loss of work time for our volunteers."

The judge motioned her forward and she provided him with the paper that presumably listed the figures.

Lorelei hadn't even thought of that. She had cost the volunteer fire department money. But still, she knew good and well that Linda had called at least twice when she thought she smelled gas, which turned out to be nothing. And Linda hadn't been called in and reproached for costing the city money over her paranoia.

She wondered if she would have to pay those expenses. How much were they? She wanted to see that paper. She had no idea how much gas it took a fire truck to drive up the street. Or that they would estimate how much it cost to keep the little station maintained and try to apply part of it to her expense.

Her belly quivered again. She had almost finished the bracelet order, but she had counted on that money to keep her in her apartment another month.

This was a hot mess. Lorelei wasn't making her way in the world at all.

Her eyes pricked with tears. This was how low

she had become, sitting in the Applebottom court-room in front of everybody while being reminded of all her failures. She should've stayed in college, no matter what.

What a ridiculous thing to do, to drop out over a boy. Gary in particular. He most certainly was not worth it.

Both Micah and the other woman spoke a couple more times, and the judge asked a few questions, but Lorelei found she couldn't pay any attention.

Her mind buzzed. What could she do now? What *should* she do? She'd used the last of her loan. She'd been expected to graduate. She only had something like twelve credit hours to go. Maybe fifteen, because she might have failed to get credit for one of her courses last fall. She'd never even looked at her last report, sure it would be terrible. She'd shut her eyes, rolled over and quit trying.

That ended today. This very afternoon, she would pull her life together.

Micah nudged her. "Lorelei, the judge is addressing you. Just like I told you he might."

Right. Micah had given her a few lines to say, but they were completely gone from her mind.

"So what is your plan, Miss Spencer?" the judge asked. He looked a little perturbed to have to ask twice.

Lorelei stood up, then remembered Micah had told her they would stay seated, that this wasn't like courtroom dramas on television where the lawyers walked around and grandstanded. So she plunked back down again.

"I'm going to call the University," she said, "and I'm going to talk to my counselor and see if I can finish my degree. I only have one semester to go. I won't be around Applebottom to cause any further problems, sir—I mean, Your Honor."

Micah didn't look at her, his attention focused on the judge.

Lorelei wondered if he was upset at her for going off script. Would that cause a problem? Had she just made things worse?

"Very well," Judge Hughes said. He picked up the sheet of paper the woman had passed to him, and adjusted his glasses to peer at it. "You will pay a fine of twenty-five dollars to cover the fuel cost of the fire truck for your call. I reckon everything else is already covered in taxes, which your family has paid to our community for many decades." He gave a quick nod to the back of the courtroom, and Lorelei was sure it was at her family.

Judge Hughes picked up his gavel. "To ensure you are reminded of the importance of the community you endangered, you will also do eight hours of court-approved community service." He paused, his expression turning a bit more stern. "I approve heartily of your decision to go back to school. Hopefully finishing your degree and finding gainful employment will get you through the setbacks we all inevitably face as we go through adult life."

Lorelei's face burned but she managed a quiet, "Thank you, Your Honor."

"Please remit the fee on your way out of court or arrange for payment," Judge Hughes said. "The administrator will provide a list of approved community service."

He banged the gavel.

It was over!

Micah and the other woman shook hands, then he began packing his things. "I'll walk you out," he said.

He slung the strap of his valise over his shoulder, and Lorelei followed him through the gate and up the aisle. The guard called another case to come forward.

Lorelei's family stood as they approached, and they all filed silently out of the courtroom. Her father peeled off to the side window, already taking his wallet out. He must be going to pay her fine.

"Well, that was something," her mother said, reaching out to adjust Lorelei's hair. "Are you really going to go back to Arkansas?"

"I'll call them this afternoon and see if they'll take me," Lorelei said. Now that she was past the moment, all the problems with her plan flashed forward. How would she pay for it? Was it too late to sign up for the fall semester? Where would she live? The dorms were bound to be full.

"We'll help you," her mother said, threading her arm through Lorelei's.

Her father shook Micah's hand. "Thank you for helping out our girl. I'm more than happy to pay your fee."

"No, no," Micah said. "I was brought in on this case by Judge Hughes' request."

"Well, at least let us buy you lunch," her father countered. "We're all headed to Annabelle's.

"That I will accept," Micah said.

As they passed through the entryway and onto the street, Micah asked, "Did you all drive in one car?"

"They brought Mandy's van," Lorelei said. "But I'll ride with you."

Her parents glanced at each other. She didn't give them a chance to protest.

"Bye!" She grabbed Micah's arm and dragged him in the direction of his office. "Get me away from them for a moment."

He grinned. "Happy to oblige."

CHAPTER 12

*M*icah realized he had not thought the entire lunch through when he arrived at Annabelle's Café to the cacophony of a full-fledged lunch hour, and a gigantic set of tables pushed together for all the members of Lorelei's family.

Normally he would take events like this in stride. But the reprimand Judge Hughes had delivered yesterday still felt fresh, particularly since he had just seen the man. It didn't seem to matter that Micah's obligation as Lorelei's attorney was over. The word *propriety* still stuck in his mind.

Lorelei's father stood up to shake Micah's hand as they approached the table.

"So glad you could be here," he said. "Thank you again."

Annabelle herself came around to take their drink

orders. When it was Lorelei's turn, she said, "Micah and I will both have sweet tea."

The table got quiet. Micah didn't miss the raised eyebrows of Lorelei's mother, or the smug satisfaction of her grandmother Betty.

He was being railroaded—but at the same time, he liked Lorelei. He had no idea whether to go with it or try to take control of the situation.

"Lorelei," her mother said. "Maybe if we knew a little more about what happened when you left U of A, we could be more helpful."

Lorelei got very still. Micah had the urge to squeeze her hand in support, but didn't dare with the whole table watching.

"I just floundered a bit," Lorelei said. "I'll get it all taken care of."

Betty accepted a tea glass from Annabelle's tray and lifted it in the air. "Of course you will, darling. Here's to the beginning of you working everything out."

As Annabelle passed around the drink order, everyone raised a glass. Micah did likewise, although he sensed that Lorelei disliked the attention at the moment.

"Hear, hear," her father said, and everyone lowered their glasses. Lorelei's shoulders relaxed.

Her mother, however, seemed unwilling to let the subject go. "I assume you'll be leaving Linda's place then, if you'll be moving back to the University."

"I don't know, Mom. I have to talk to them first."

"I don't see any reason why they wouldn't accept you back." Her mother glanced around the table. "I'm an alum, and so is your father, and your Uncle Sam. They have to take you back."

Micah could feel Lorelei vibrating with nervous tension beside him. He stopped Annabelle as she passed with her empty tray. "Annabelle, please tell me you have some peach cobbler back there. Today might be the sort of day I want to have dessert first."

"You'll have no such thing until you've got something solid in your belly," Annabelle scolded him.

The table laughed and the attention switched away from Lorelei. Betty followed his lead by talking about peach cobblers she remembered from her childhood, and soon the discussion was off and running.

Micah twitched a little with surprise when Lorelei's hand found his wrist below the table and squeezed it, just as he had contemplated doing to her a few minutes before. When he glanced over at her, she mouthed the words *thank you*.

Annabelle's patrons knew that a large party that seemed to want to sit around and talk might languish while she dealt with the smaller groups on their lunch break. Micah spent a good hour listening and observing the extended Spencer family while Annabelle doled out appetizers.

It was an interesting dynamic to watch. Micah

had never felt like an outsider in his own family, but then, it had been a family of outsiders. His father worked long hours, and his mother preferred the company of social climbing women from the nearby city over the small-town friendships found in Applebottom.

Micah and Josh had been close, in the rough-and-tumble way brothers can often be. Micah scarcely knew his father's parents, as his grandfather was a lawyer in Sacramento. It was his maternal grand-mother who'd kept them in Applebottom for so long. Widowed at a young age with a single young daughter, she had guilted Micah's mother about going too far away.

So Micah's father had set up practice in Applebot-tom, and even when his mother-in-law passed on, he found the small town life to his liking. He always said, "Far enough away from the rat race, but close enough to an airport."

All they knew now was airports. Micah hadn't seen his parents in months. They'd even skipped Christmas. But then, holidays were always the hardest.

The food arrived, but before everyone began eating, Betty suggested that Micah say grace.

Another little Applebottom test. Micah joined hands with the others, Lorelei's soft warm one, and Betty's fragile, birdlike bones.

He could do this all day. He gave thanks for a

successful day in court, for the gathering of family, and for this wonderful establishment. And at the end, he added, "And please provide peach cobbler for dear Betty." A gentle laugh circled the table.

"So charming," Lorelei's mother said as they all reached for their forks. "Micah, did you ever meet my father, Betty's husband? He was a charmer too."

"Didn't he used to teach us how to square dance in elementary for pioneer day?" Micah asked.

"Oh, yes, he loved doing that," Betty said. "In fact, Lorelei was quite good at it. Nowadays we have a Sock Hop on Saturday nights listening to Elvis Presley."

"I believe I knew that," Micah said. "We had a meeting the other day, and Lorelei was listening to, what was it?"

"Jail House Rock," Lorelei said, her voice low.

This caused an uproar at the table. When the laughter subsided, Betty said, "You know, I heard that there's a Sock Hop happening in Branson this weekend. They have an Elvis impersonator and everything."

"Do you like Elvis, Micah?" Lorelei's mother asked.

"I think he's fine," Micah said. "He's classic."

"Lorelei, you have to go," her mother said. "Maybe you can take your grandmother."

"Oh, no, I could never make it out that late," Betty said. "But I agree that Lorelei should go." And without batting an eyelash, she turned right to Micah and said, "Would you take her, Micah? You two seem to get along."

Micah glanced around the table. The men had all stopped eating, their eyes big. Even Lorelei's mom seemed a little aghast at Betty's audacity.

He was afraid to look at Lorelei.

"Oh, Grandma," Lorelei said. "Don't try to strong-arm him into taking me somewhere."

Betty was undeterred. "Bud," she said to Lorelei's father. "You get on your phone right now and buy two tickets to that Sock Hop for your daughter and this young man."

Bud looked from his mother-in-law to his daughter, then rested his eyes on Micah. "I'm not sure –"

"Hogwash," Betty said. "You will do it right now."

Lorelei's father pulled his phone out of his pocket. "All righty, then. Two tickets to the Branson Sock Hop with an Elvis impersonator."

Micah finally managed to turn to Lorelei. Her face was white. *I'm sorry*, she mouthed.

All Micah could do was laugh. He didn't know exactly how this town had done it, but somehow they had managed to finagle a date between him and Lorelei Spencer.

CHAPTER 13

"Grandma, ouch!" Lorelei's hands reached for her head, but she managed to stop herself before she wrecked the perfect row of curlers her grandmother had aligned on her head.

"Sit still, child," Grandma Betty chided. "I haven't seen you this wiggly since you had to wait your turn to be the angel in the church Christmas play."

"It was a lot of pressure, announcing the birth of Jesus," Lorelei said. "And you guys practically forced the town lawyer to go on a date with me tonight."

"We didn't make that boy do anything he didn't already want to do."

"How do you know that?" Lorelei winced as another curler came out. These Velcro rollers were not her favorite. Her hair always seemed to get tangled in them. But Grandma Betty had insisted.

"There are some things a grandmother just

knows," Grandma Betty said. "Did you know that Judge Hughes called him out for going down to the dock with you while he was still your attorney? And he didn't even flinch. And the judge moved up your hearing just so he could go to this."

Lorelei turned to her grandmother incredulously. "You guys planned this?"

Grandma Betty turned Lorelei's head back around. "Just two more curlers to go. Sit still now. I'm not saying we did, and I'm not saying we didn't. I just had no idea about this whole attorney-client rule. Thankfully, the judge was able to move things up."

"So when you told Daddy to buy the tickets…" Lorelei had a feeling she knew what her grandmother was about to say.

"They were already bought. It was just for show."

Lorelei would have held her face in her hands, if her grandmother hadn't been tugging on her hair. "I can get my own dates, Grandma."

"You were mooning over that other boy who was not worth his britches," she said, "so we had to make you snap out of it."

"What if he doesn't really want to do this? A Sock Hop isn't exactly a coffee date."

"Don't fret. He's doing it for you."

Lorelei looked over at her outfit, which hung on the back of Grandma Betty's bedroom closet. A glorious pink satin skirt adorned with a black poodle precisely matched a sweater with a white sweetheart collar. Black-and-white saddle shoes, shined and buffed until they looked almost new, waited on a chair with a pair of little white ankle socks.

Grandma started brushing out the curls.

"What are you doing to my hair again?"

"Well, if you'd let me cut your hair, we would've done the most perfect flip ever put on a girl."

"Grandma…"

"I know, you like it long. So we're curling it up as tight as we can, adding a little volume to the front, and putting it in a high ponytail that will swing in one continuous, perfect curl."

They'd already done her makeup. A heavy stroke crossed the edge of her eyelid, sweeping up on the edges. Her lips were bright pink and perfectly shiny, a match for her skirt. And she sported a tiny black beauty mark just to the side of her upper lip.

Her grandmother had laid out a pair of white pearl earrings and a matching white choker.

"I put some Dr. Scholl's in those saddle shoes to make sure you can dance all night," Grandma Betty said. "I distinctly recall how much my feet hurt after a night in those."

Lorelei concentrated on not letting her eyes tear up as her grandmother brushed through the curls over and over again to get them to wave together. It seemed that Grandma Betty might be a little nervous herself.

Finally, her grandmother stepped back. "My sweet, you are a picture."

Lorelei hurried to the bathroom mirror. She barely recognized herself, a relic from a bygone era. "Do you think I need blush?" she asked.

"Oh, no," Betty said. "Eyes and lips only." She passed Lorelei the outfit. "Hurry along now. He'll be here very soon."

Micah would be on time. Lorelei knew that much.

She quickly stepped into the outfit. It was authentic. All these items, other than the socks, had belonged to Grandma Betty. She was the exact same size her grandmother had been—although, by the time Betty was twenty-four, she was already married and expecting her first child.

When Lorelei emerged from the bathroom, Grandma Betty clapped her hands.

"You are a picture," she said. "Let me get my camera."

Lorelei smiled, knowing that Grandma Betty would indeed go get an actual camera. She was never completely convinced that a cell phone would actually take a picture you could use.

Lorelei had just finished tying the second shoe when she heard a knock at the door.

"There he is!" Grandma Betty said from the hall.

She heard Betty greeting Micah at the door, and turned to the mirror one more time. She smoothed the sweater and made sure it was well tucked in. The dress flared out from the waist, courtesy of the crinoline skirt underneath. She twirled, laughing at the little pink hotpants underneath them that her grandmother had insisted on. She was right. These skirts flew all the way up if she turned fast enough. Did Micah dance? She had no idea.

"Lorelei, are you ready?" Grandma Betty called.

Lorelei picked up her phone and tucked it inside a tiny clutch purse with a wrist strap. She walked down the hall and into the living room, then stopped short when she saw Micah.

He had gone all out as a greaser.

His dark hair was shiny and combed straight up, twirling into a perfect curl in the center of his forehead. He wore a white T-shirt with a pack of cigarettes rolled into one sleeve, or at least something the right size and shape.

And he'd shaved his beard!

"Your beard!" she said.

"Are you sad? I can grow it back. It didn't fit the look."

"He's right," Grandma Betty said.

"I like it both ways." Lorelei surveyed him, the strong jaw, the smooth cheeks. "Definitely both ways."

His blue jeans were rolled up at the ankle. He held a black leather jacket slung over his shoulder.

"You look perfect," Lorelei said.

He gestured at her. "Not as perfect as you. Wow. Just, wow."

Grandma Betty beamed. "You two are the spitting image of my glory days."

Micah turned in a quick circle, like a dancer.

Lorelei had to take a step back. Who was this guy? She had never seen him move like that.

Grandma Betty clapped her hands together. "Let's get some pictures!"

Betty had actually gotten out her old Polaroid and took some shots that they shook in the air to process, then lined up on the back of the sofa.

"You ready?" Micah asked. "I have a little surprise outside."

Lorelei and Grandma Betty looked at each other as Micah opened the door.

But then they saw it.

Sitting on the curb in its shiny waxed glory, was a blue-and-white 1957 Chevrolet.

"Oh, my word," Grandma Betty said. "I haven't seen one of these in forty years."

"It's Archie's," Micah said. "He restores cars and was willing to let me take one out for the night."

"Go stand by it," Betty said. "I have to take more pictures."

"You really knocked it out of the park," Lorelei said to Micah.

"Might as well go all in," he said.

Indeed. Lorelei felt her stomach turn over. She

had worried that Micah would find the whole evening to be a big drag. But he had really stepped up.

She had a feeling that she was in for the night of her life.

&a.

When Micah pulled up to the dance hall, the Sock Hop was obviously already in full swing. Colored lights flashed inside the building, and the thump of the bass could be heard even outdoors.

As Micah opened his door, two teen girls in poodle skirts ran up to his car with a squeal.

"Can we take a picture with your car?" one asked. "It's so perfect!"

"Of course," Micah said. He'd figured that would happen.

He got out of the way and circled the car to Lorelei.

"I think the car is a hit!" she said.

He extended a hand, and she took it as she stepped out. The two girls let out another squeal, then ran toward the building.

Micah and Lorelei walked hand-in-hand toward the lights and sound. The low squat building had once been a skating rink. Micah had been to it a time or two when he was young.

"I'm so excited!" Lorelei said.

"I think it will be fun," Micah said. In truth, he'd never done anything like this before. It was the sort of thing the crowds that he'd run with would have sneered at. They tended to stick to pursuits that involved club seats or VIP rooms or backstage meet and greets, expecting that either their prestige or their money would set them apart.

Judging from the enthusiasm of the people hurrying up to the door to participate in the Sock Hop, Micah wondered how much he'd missed by ascribing to their elitist philosophy.

Possibly quite a lot.

A friendly, balding man in a retro bowling outfit sat on a stool just inside the door.

"You ready for a rocking good time?" he asked as he took their tickets.

"It will be dynamite," Lorelei said.

"Right on," the man said.

They entered a big open area with a snack bar and little cubbies where skaters used to keep their shoes. Quite a few people hung out here, many in poodle skirts, but others in form-fitting pants that were cropped near the knee. There were many pairs of cats-eye glasses, and some of the women had their hair piled high on their head.

Most of the men sported a combination of T-shirts and jeans, although a few wore suits that were clearly hand-me-downs from grandparents. A few dressed on the nerd end of the spectrum in sweater vests and horn-rimmed glasses.

"Should we get a locker for your jacket and my purse?" Lorelei asked. "It's too warm in here for leather." She pointed to a line of steel lockers where you could lock your belongings.

"Sure," he said.

When they had secured their things, he took her hand and they headed into the flashing lights of the main dance floor.

A stage had been erected on one end, and a five-piece band in old-fashioned suits played a slow dance.

Dozens of couples melded together to a song Micah recognized as "Blue Moon."

"Shall we?" he asked Lorelei, gesturing to the floor. The song had an entire verse left.

He noted her surprise, almost as if she must have thought he couldn't, or wouldn't, dance.

"Yes!" she said. "I'd love to!"

When he took Lorelei in his arms, they immediately fell into step together. A sense of harmony flowed through him as they moved. He could smell the faint traces of her hair spray, a hint of floral hand lotion, and underlying it, the smell of just her, which he realized he now recognized in some deep part of himself.

As the song went on, she relaxed against him. Both her arms drifted up to his shoulders and clasped behind his neck. He held her lightly at the waist, enjoying the rhythm of their dance steps working in unison.

She felt good in his arms. There was no artifice here, nothing to prove. She didn't put on any airs, or strike a pose. She was an entirely different sort of woman than he'd been around before. He did not want to mess this up.

All too soon, the song came to an end. As the couples parted and clapped for the band, they all turned toward the stage.

The drum began to beat faster, then a guitar kicked in, then another. The energy began to rise, and all around them, the dancers stomped their feet.

A roll of smoke shot across the stage floor, and Lorelei turned to him, her eyebrows lifted, a crazy grin on her face.

He nodded at her, continuing to clap along. He'd never experienced anything like this. Sure, he'd been to rock concerts. And definitely other musical events. But this felt different. He was actually a part of it.

The anticipation built for another moment, then from the side of the stage, a figure emerged from the rising pool of fog.

It was a man dressed in a white costume covered with gold rhinestones. He had a full head of jet-black hair and long sideburns. Oversized aviator glasses covered his eyes. He carried a white guitar, and when he stepped forward into the light, the crowd went crazy.

If they cleared their minds for just a moment, if they forgot what year it was and got lost in a decade long past, they would totally have believed that Elvis had just entered the building.

CHAPTER 14

*L*orelei's heart hammered as the Elvis impersonator greeted the crowd with, "Thank you very much."

The audience roared. She reached for Micah's hand and squeezed it. Everything about this evening had been perfect so far. The way they had slow danced. His enthusiastic response to everything.

"I'm going to open tonight with a song that is near and dear to my heart," Elvis continued. "I think it will get you fired up and ready to rock 'n' roll."

As soon as he started the opening lick, the crowd went crazy. Micah gripped her hand and pulled her toward him, then spun her back out again.

Hey! He could really dance!

They leapt right into the rhythm of the song, shifting their feet and twirling back and forth.

Lorelei wanted to giggle with glee. This was nuts.

Nothing she'd ever done in her grandmother's living room had felt quite like this.

As Elvis crooned his way to the title line, "All Shook Up," Micah expertly spun her around, even lifting her by the waist.

Each song ran directly into the next, "Jail House Rock," "Hound Dog," "Blue Suede Shoes." Only when Elvis brought the tempo down and started talking over the gentle strum of the guitar, did Lorelei realize how much time had passed.

"This is crazy fun," she said to Micah.

He nodded, fitting behind her, her back against his chest, as they listened to what Elvis had to say.

His embrace was so familiar, so comfortable. No night with Gary had ever felt like this.

"Ladies and gentlemen," Elvis said. "I'm looking out at a lot of beautiful people tonight." He paused as some of the crowd screamed in response.

"I'm going to play another song for you, and if you fellas have a lady at your side, pull her close, because tonight is about to get magical."

The lighting shifted, and instead of spots of color, everything twinkled with white. The crowd *oohed* and *aahed*, and the first gentle notes began to play of a song everyone was familiar with: "Love Me Tender."

Lorelei turned around to face Micah. He looked so perfect in this soft light. His hair had not completely held its greaser curl, and had fallen back into a more normal sweep. His eyebrows were thick and expressive, and his jaw strong.

He moved his hands back to her waist, and she returned her arms to their position around his neck.

The rest of the room fell away as Elvis began to sing.

Lorelei couldn't stop looking into Micah's eyes. He stared back down at her, his expression solemn. All around, couples danced close together, letting the lights and the music fill the space.

Micah had become so familiar over the last couple of weeks. As much as Lorelei hated to admit it, Grandma Betty had been right. Micah did want to be here with her. She could see it in his expression, and how he held her.

Something shifted inside her. Why had she thought that her life was over because some guy had jilted her? He hadn't even been the *right* guy.

She wasn't sure how things would work with Micah, especially if she was going to leave for college. But tonight, this felt exactly right.

As the slow dance came to an end, and they moved back into a faster tempo, they walked off the dance floor to grab a soda and a malted shake. But the sense of rightness never left her.

They stayed at the Sock Hop all the way to the end, until the final number played.

She really didn't want this night to be over.

But by the time he walked her up to the outer

door of Linda's house, it was almost two in the morning. There was nowhere else to go.

"That was really fun," Micah said.

"It was," she said. She smoothed the satin of her poodle skirt. She hoped Grandma Betty would let her keep it. She felt extraordinarily attached to the outfit.

She plucked at the sleeve of his T-shirt and unrolled the little box that had served as a pack of smokes.

When she saw what had actually been inside, she laughed. "Candy cigarettes?"

"Now you know my dark secret," he said. "Sugar addiction."

"You really going to eat these?"

He laughed. "Probably not." He passed them to her. "You keep them."

Lorelei hugged the small box against her chest. They looked at each other a little longer, still wanting to linger in the glow of the evening.

"So," he said, "now that our attorney-client relationship is over, I suppose we could do this again. Maybe something of our own choosing."

Lorelei washed over with happiness. "I would like that."

"I'm not sure I can top this as far as your favorite things, though."

"I think just being with you is enough."

His mouth quirked into a little half-grin. "I think I feel exactly the same way."

"I hate it when the town is right about something."

Micah laughed. "You gotta hand it to them."

They stood there another moment more, and Lorelei held her breath. Would he kiss her? Like he said, it was perfectly allowed now, and the town had practically given their blessing. In fact, she half-expected Grandma Betty to pop up with the camera to take a picture of it if they did. The thought of it made her smile.

"What funny thing is crossing your mind?" he asked.

"I'm just picturing someone trying to capture this moment with a Polaroid."

"This moment?"

"A first kiss," she said, and then her face bloomed warm.

"Is that what happens next?"

"I sure hope so," she said. "But I might be a little forward for a girl from 1957."

"I like it," he said. And he leaned forward, closing the distance between them.

Her eyes closed as his lips brushed against hers.

The rush of emotion she had felt repeatedly that night crashed over her again. Elvis sang in her head, crooning the words of "Love Me Tender."

She had a feeling she might soon be able to do exactly that.

CHAPTER 15

*M*icah tried to quell his annoyance as he drove out of Branson late afternoon on Monday. The day had been scheduled end-to-end with meetings, but a ridiculous number of clients had been late. Now he was stuck in five o'clock traffic, and he wanted nothing more than to get home.

As he sat through the third cycle of the light that was still several intersections away from the freeway, Micah spotted a *grand opening* sign at a shop on the corner.

Below, it read *Romantic Picnic Basket Meals.*

Micah glanced at the time. Traffic was not going to die down for another half hour at least.

He wondered what Lorelei would think of a romantic picnic basket dinner.

He inched forward a couple feet, then punched

the contact list built into his car's hands-free phone system.

He pressed Lorelei's name and waited as the call connected.

"Micah?" Lorelei's voice came over his speaker. "Is that you?"

"Yeah. I'm in my car in Branson."

"What are you doing in Branson? Looking for another Sock Hop?"

"Heh. Maybe. I had meetings all day. Listen, I just spotted this cute new little business that has picnic dinners packed in baskets. And I was wondering if I should stop and pick one up. You down for doing a picnic dinner? We could go to my parents' dock, behind their lake house. Fewer onlookers than at the park."

"Sure!" she said. "Anything to escape the prying eyes of my crazy family."

"We're on. By the time I get this packed up and all the way back to Applebottom, it'll probably be closer to seven."

"That's fine. I'll meet you at your parents' lake house at seven-thirty?"

"Sounds good. I'll let you know if I get behind."

"See you then."

He killed the call and turned into the parking lot of the shop. He hoped they could pack a decent dinner. But he liked trying out new things. And even in Branson, new wasn't always easy to come by.

Any excuse to see Lorelei.

As Lorelei drove up to the enormous lake house, a little rush of nerves zipped through her belly. She'd called Mandy about this invitation, because she knew her sister had been out to the Livingston's lake house at least once.

Mandy chided her for not talking about Micah with her before now. "But I forgive you. Just know that the house is super fancy, super clean, sort of like a mausoleum. You'll be afraid to wear shoes on the spiffy floors."

"I thought they had a million crazy parties out there," Lorelei said.

"They did. And they had a cleaning staff come right afterward to take care of everything."

"Well, it's just going to be me and Micah."

"Good. Because that party scene was way crazy."

Lorelei didn't want to linger on Micah's wild past, since her sister might bring it up with their parents, so she changed the subject. "How is my nephew percolating?"

"He's a kicker. We'll have him on the soccer team by the time he's five."

"That'll be fun. You'll be a soccer mom! I'll call you tomorrow."

"Have fun, and Lorelei—"

"Yeah?"

"Be careful. Micah runs in a very different crowd."

"Okay."

As Lorelei sat looking up at the outrageous two-story house that was difficult to see from the road, she could believe it. She'd been too young to go to Micah's parties, and this was overwhelming. Enormous columns framed a huge entryway. A circle drive could hold dozens of cars.

She was out of her league. Big time.

But he'd kissed her. They weren't talking about court anymore, because the case was over.

Time to see if they were more than a good time at a Sock Hop.

When Micah opened the door, he was dressed super casually in shorts and a T-shirt.

And he held a tiny brown Chihuahua in his arms like a football.

"Who is this?" she asked, reaching out to pet the little dog's head.

"Chief," Micah said. "Technically, he's my mom's dog. Most of the time he stays here with Maya, who keeps the place running while my parents are away."

Lorelei stepped inside. "Is Maya here?"

"No, she takes off Monday evening through Wednesday morning of every week. That's why this little guy is mine tonight." He lifted the dog.

"Well, he's adorable."

Micah closed the front door and set down Chief,

who immediately began running around Lorelei's feet.

"Now, Chief," Micah said. "Be on good behavior for Lorelei."

Chief paid him no mind, continuing to run in frenzied circles.

Lorelei laughed. "We had a few chihuahuas growing up," she said. "They are definitely active little dogs."

"He'll settle down in a minute," Micah said.

Lorelei took a moment to look around. Mandy had been right. This place was crazy big, and everything shined.

The foyer was lined with beautiful sandy-brown tile, and the walls were dark beige with white trim. A white staircase led upstairs, and enormous paintings filled the towering walls. In the center of the entryway, a large marble table held a gigantic arrangement of flowers.

"I think you could fit my entire section of Linda's house in this entryway," Lorelei said.

"Yeah, well, it's not so great when it's empty and echoing," Micah said.

They passed beneath the stairs and into a bright stainless steel kitchen that looked like it could support a small restaurant. A pretty wicker basket sat on the center island.

"Is this the purchase you made today?" she asked.

"Yes, they were really great. They had tons of food options and it all sounded really delicious."

"Can I peek?"

He lifted the lid of the basket.

Inside was a little section with two plates, silverware, two glasses and a pair of cloth napkins.

"It came with plates and things?"

"It was an add-on. I thought it would go well with the basket just to stay in there."

She nodded. An insulated section had to be unzipped. She opened it. Inside were containers with croissant sandwiches, two salads, and a bowl of mixed berries. Another bowl held pasta salad with olives. And tucked on the side was an extra large slice of lemon meringue pie.

Lorelei looked up. "Don't let Gertrude and Maude find out you bought pie from someone else."

"I wouldn't dream of it. They'd run me out of town." Micah closed the lid and lifted the basket off the counter. "There's some water bottles at the bottom. Did you want anything else?"

"No, that sounds perfect."

They walked to the back door, then he stopped. "Oh. The dock might be a little uncomfortable to sit on. Let me see if there's a blanket or picnic tablecloth or something."

He set the basket down and turned to a large door in the corner. When he opened it, Lorelei had to take a step back. This was no pantry. This was the storage area of a five-star restaurant.

He disappeared inside, and Lorelei walked a little closer, lost in awe. Every kind of food imaginable lined the shelves. Cans and boxes and packages. Sacks of flour. Who needed a sack of flour? An entire section was devoted to various flavored waters. Another section held at least six different kinds of coffee. Installed on a small table was a coffee grinder like you might see in a store.

Lorelei shook her head, and her stomach flipped again. She was way out of her depth here.

Micah searched through a cabinet in the back and produced a red and white checkered cloth. "Voilà," he said.

She followed him to the back door, where he scooped up the basket and they headed outside. Chief followed them out, his tiny nails clicking on the tile.

The evening was quiet and serene. A large covered porch held a couple tables with wicker chairs. Then a stone path led through the grass and down the rocks to a long dock.

Attached to the dock was a boat house. Lorelei's sandals clomped on the wood planks as they crossed above the rocky ledge and over the water.

They were at the height of summer, the longest days of the year. The sun wouldn't set for another hour. But the heat of the day had mostly burned off, and the air was just starting to resound with a chorus of cicadas beneath the dock.

Micah set the basket down and unfolded the blanket. "Is this okay? Not too hot?"

"It's perfect."

She kicked off her sandals and sat on one corner of the blanket. Micah settled next to her and dragged the basket closer. "Josh and I used to come out here all the time and throw rocks," he said. "We could just sit out here for hours and not say a word."

Lorelei knew what he meant. "Mandy and I can do the same thing. Although I'm kind of a talker, so the silence doesn't usually go on too long."

Micah laughed, digging through the basket until he produced two bottles of water. "That's all right. I could probably use some of my silence filled."

"You live by yourself?" she asked, although she was pretty sure he did.

"I have since I've been back here. I tried living with my parents at first, but that very quickly became a bad idea. They never called when they were going to return from one of their trips, so inevitably they would show up without warning. I nearly clubbed my own father with a fireplace poker."

"Oh! Did they start calling ahead after that?"

"Nope. I bought a little house of my own. But when I'm here, I set the lighting to blink three times if the code is pushed so I can tell the difference between them and a burglar."

Chief curled up in one corner of the blanket.

"I don't think I've ever met your parents," Lorelei said. "Although I'm sure we've been at the same events. Harvest Dance. One of the Centennials."

"Probably," Micah said. "They weren't always ones to hobnob with the locals, although my dad worked with lots of people in town."

Lorelei opened her water bottle and stared out at the lake, sparkling in the early evening sun. This was the life, for sure.

Micah pulled out plates and loaded them with food. The croissant sandwiches looked even more delectable outside of their packaging, and Lorelei could think of nothing more romantic than what they were doing, sitting on the dock on this beautiful lake and having a picnic. She was the luckiest girl in the world.

As they ate, Micah pulled out a chicken chunk from his sandwich and fed it to Chief. Watching Micah with the tiny dog brought on a gentle feeling inside Lorelei. How could this man be any more perfect?

They worked their way through the contents of the basket, talking amicably about the Sock Hop, Judge Hughes, Annabelle and her café, and some of the other prominent locals in Applebottom.

The conversation was easy, because they had their whole lives in common. The difference in their ages only served to give them a different perspective about the same people and events.

"I don't know what happened at the Last Ditch the years you were there," Lorelei said. "But when I was a senior, they threatened to get rid of it because too many girls cried that nobody asked them to the dance. The principal had to shut it down."

Micah shook his head. "They threaten to end it every year for one reason or another. When I was a junior, the Last Ditch went so long, that they had to hold the school buses."

"Well, they're still doing it," Lorelei said. "I guess it's nothing but idle threats."

"At least the football team is good now," Micah said. "Back in my day, they couldn't even score a touchdown."

"My day either," Lorelei said. "It's sorta not fair. Now the cheerleaders have something to cheer about."

"Were you a cheerleader?"

Lorelei tilted her head and looked away. "Maybe I was, maybe I wasn't."

Micah laughed. "Oh, man. So that's why you like being a paper shaker."

"Oh!" Lorelei gasped in mock indignation. "Are you judging me for my school spirit?"

Micah laughed. "I wouldn't dare. I think it's cute."

The sun had started to dip in the horizon, so a

sudden flood of lights from the house startled them both.

Micah jumped to his feet, then the lights blinked three times.

"Your parents?" Lorelei asked. "I assume you weren't expecting them."

"Nope. Although maybe Maya came back for something. She'd use the code too."

Micah began striding swiftly toward the house. "You stay here just in case."

At his tone, Chief jumped up and began to bark. Lorelei picked up the dog. He was shaking.

"It's okay," Lorelei assured the dog. "I'm sure it's nothing."

Micah had only made it halfway to the house when the back door opened, and a woman came out.

Lorelei couldn't quite make her out from this distance, as she was silhouetted in the light.

But Micah stopped dead in his tracks.

Another figure came out the back door, this one a man. He had a bold confident stride that resembled how Micah walked.

So it was his parents. They were home.

Now she was nervous. She hadn't dreamed she would be meeting Micah's family this quickly. And how did it look to them, the two of them alone at their lake house?

She felt sick. This wasn't how she wanted it to happen at all.

She continued to stand there, stroking Chief while Micah spoke with his parents. After a moment, Micah turned and headed back her direction. His parents went inside.

"They wanted to surprise me," he said. "Apparently they planned something this weekend for my birthday."

Oh, no. "Your birthday is this weekend?"

He shrugged. "Yeah. Friday. It's no big deal."

This was the worst. There should be a rule that no major holiday, Christmas, a birthday, or heaven forbid, Valentine's Day, could fall too early in a new relationship. She hadn't even thought to ask about his birthday. They had barely even begun to see each other.

She held on to Chief like a lifeline, squeezing him so hard that eventually he started squirming to be let down.

"Should I leave?" Lorelei asked.

"No, no. We can stay out here. The sunset is amazing."

They settled back down on the picnic blanket, but everything felt different. Micah seemed tense and annoyed. Lorelei was completely beside herself with nerves. Maybe they would walk around the house and she wouldn't have to actually meet his parents.

Her thoughts whirled round and round in her head.

Eventually, the sun did set, and Micah began

packing the plates and empty containers back in the basket.

Lorelei helped, cursing their bad luck on this. Date number two was feeling like a bust.

They stood up, and Micah shook the blanket out.

"I guess we should go inside," he said. "I haven't seen my parents in months."

"Should I just leave? I'm sure you guys have a lot to catch up on."

"No, it's fine. They'll want to meet you."

Would they? Lorelei straightened her sweater and shorts self-consciously. What if she had food in her teeth? And her hair! It was a disaster after sitting in the breeze and humidity of the lake.

And she was sweaty.

This could not be happening.

Chief scrabbled alongside them as they came to the end of the dock and walked up the stone steps to the house. An impending sense of doom pressed down on Lorelei as if she were being suffocated.

Relax. They're just parents.

Rich parents. Well-connected parents. Parents she'd never met despite growing up in this town.

Did they know about her court case? Mortification flooded Lorelei. She prayed, prayed hard that no one had informed them about her struggles, and that Micah wouldn't mention it.

Surely not.

But that was how they'd met. Would this not be the first question?

Her head felt like it would burst with her worries as Micah opened the back door and stepped aside to let her go in.

Really? Did she have to go first?

She tried to take calming breath.

A petite Hispanic woman stood by the sink. This was not the woman she had seen in silhouette. "Sweet Micah, boy," the woman said. "Did you see your parents?"

"Yeah. They came out on the dock. They called you in to work on your night off?"

Lorelei deduced that this must be Maya.

"They did, but it is no problem. I will take off another day."

Chief jumped at her knees, and she bent down to pick him up, her face breaking out into a huge smile. "How is my little puppy dog?" She peered up at Micah. "When are you going to introduce me to your girl?"

Micah dropped the tablecloth on the counter. "This is Lorelei. She grew up here in Applebottom. She's Bud and Mary's daughter. Her grandmother Betty runs the tea shop on the square."

"Of course," Maya said. "What a lovely girl. Nice to meet you."

"Nice to meet you too," Lorelei said, her anxiety calming down a little. At least Maya was nice and pleased to meet her.

"I am so happy to see a girl around." Maya nudged Micah with her shoulder. "It's been too long."

Had it? A trickle of relief flowed through her.

"Did you know they were coming?" Micah asked.

"No," she said, nuzzling the dog. "They called me just a half-hour ago. Apparently they want to have a party this weekend for your thirtieth. It will take some doing to pull that off."

"Yeah, they didn't ask me about it."

Thirty. It wasn't just any birthday, but a big one. Lorelei wished she'd asked.

Maya set Chief on the floor. "Parents don't need permission to celebrate their sons. I already made you a cake. But apparently now I will have to make a bigger one. Sixty-five people, they said."

"Sixty-five." Micah shook his head. "And they didn't even check to see if I already had plans."

"Do you?" Maya glanced at Lorelei again.

"No. I don't. I just didn't want a party."

"You best go see to them," she said. "Maybe you can talk them out of it."

"It sounds like they've already invited people."

"Go and see." She began unpacking the basket. "Nice to meet you," she said to Lorelei.

Micah took Lorelei's hand and squeezed it. "All right. Let's get this over with."

Over with? Lorelei's anxiety spiked again.

They passed back through into the grand entry-way, and Micah led them to a well-lit room.

It was a study, decorated very similarly to the office Micah used for his law practice. A man, the spitting image of Micah, only perhaps thirty years his senior, sat behind a grand mahogany desk.

Micah's mother, elegant in a perfect white sheath dress, white high heels, and with glamorously styled black hair, sat on the sofa, sorting through a pile of mail.

They both glanced up as Micah knocked on the door frame.

"Mom, Dad, this is Lorelei."

His mother set aside the packet of letters and stood. She was incredibly tall, at least four inches taller than Lorelei, although a lot of that might have been the heels.

She extended a hand. "Nice to meet you," she said. "You can call me Alicia."

Lorelei shook her hand. Everything about this woman was impeccable, from the gorgeous rings on her hand to the bracelets that slid to her wrist. Her makeup was perfect. You would never know that they had been traveling that day.

"That's David," Alicia said, gesturing to the desk. "He's already elbow-deep in work." She glanced at her son. "I think we're going to be here rather indefinitely, so if there are some cases that you need your father to consult on, let him know. He'll need something to do."

"What's the occasion?" Micah said. "You haven't stayed for more than a few days in three years."

"Well it's your birthday, of course," she said. "We wanted to throw a party this year. We suspected you might be ignoring the big three-o."

"It isn't necessary," Micah said. He pulled Lorelei close to him. "I planned something small."

Alicia looked from Lorelei to Micah and back to Lorelei. "Well, you'll just have to take a rain check on that. Because we will be having a party, and I've already extended an invitation to some of our most important clients, as well as a few of your friends from law school that I managed to track down."

"You didn't have to do that," Micah said.

"It was no bother at all." Her face crumpled in an expression of concern that Lorelei didn't quite believe. "I do hope it's okay that we invited Angelique. I wasn't sure."

"She won't come," Micah said.

"Are you sure? Because she already accepted."

Who was Angelique? She had to be an old girlfriend. This was the worst. Lorelei wanted the beautiful tile beneath her to split open so that she fell through the cracks.

Alicia put on a false smile. "Of course, I had no idea that you were seeing a sweet little local girl."

Her tone was so condescending that it took

everything in Lorelei's bones to stop from make a biting retort. This was Micah's mother. She would have to stay the course and be calm.

"I'll handle it," Micah said.

"You can't un-invite her," Alicia said. "That would be terribly rude."

"I'll handle it," Micah said again.

"Of course your little friend should come," Alicia said.

Lorelei's internal combustion engine chugged to a new level of red. *Little friend. Little local girl.*

She took in a deep breath and let it out slowly.

Micah noticed. He squeezed her hand.

"Come on, Lorelei. I'll walk you to your car."

"Nice meeting you!" Alicia said, her smile falsely bright.

"Bye," Micah's father called from his desk. He had not bothered to get up.

Lorelei had never felt more inconsequential in her entire life.

Not even when Gary left her.

"Nice to meet you, too," she managed to get out.

Micah led her out the front door and to her car.

She didn't want to tell him how mortified she was, although it was tempting. Would this be the end of their relationship right here?

Maybe so. His parents obviously weren't impressed by her.

She tried to open her car door, but Micah said, "Hey."

He turned her toward him. "Don't let them get to you. Their method of coping with the world is by intimidation. That's their way. Not mine."

He pulled her against him, and she laid her head on his shoulder.

They were so new. Everything was new. All she knew about him was what she had seen in the last two weeks. That he was a fire fighter. That he was good at his job. That he cared about the community. And that he liked her.

She pictured him in his 1950s outfit. He'd done that for her. She remembered their kiss on Linda's doorstep and tried to calm down.

Micah pulled away just an inch, and lifted her chin with his finger. "I'm still me, right? Please don't judge me by them."

Lorelei realized he was right. "You are amazing," she said.

"So are you," he said. "They'll come around. You're really just getting the brunt of me not having told them about you. They don't like surprises."

"That makes sense."

"So are we okay?"

"We're okay."

He leaned in to kiss her, and she relaxed against his chest. His lips were soft and gentle, a sort of apology. But also a reminder. They were good together. They would see this through.

When they broke apart, she asked, "So, when is your birthday exactly?"

"Friday," he said. "Though I'm guessing the party will be Saturday."

"Should I go?"

"Of course you should," he said. "I won't hear of you not coming."

"Okay," she said.

He squeezed her hand and let go. As she got into her car and backed out of the elaborate driveway with the intimidating stone gates, her first thought was *wait until I tell my sister about this.*

CHAPTER 16

Micah's birthday had already been better than any he remembered.

Lorelei showed up at his office with lunch and a little cake she'd made in her grandmother's shop. She'd even had Betty's top-notch cake decorator create a tiny version of Chief on top.

They'd made plans for dinner in Branson that night, sneaking in a little alone time before the big birthday bash the next evening.

Micah found himself whistling as he collected his things at the end of the day. For the first time in a while, his birthday wasn't immediately bringing back negative feelings about who wouldn't be there to celebrate with him anymore. There was no doubt that the last few years had involved subdued celebrations on all counts, knowing Josh would not be with them.

But things were feeling different. His parents had come home to throw a birthday party. As annoyed as he was that he had not been given any prior warning, this did mean that they were doing better.

And Lorelei improved everything. She was spunky and funny and real. He'd never dated anyone like her. Surviving his mother's cold perusal proved she had some mettle.

As he walked the few blocks to his modest house just off the square, he suddenly remembered he hadn't dealt with the issue of Angelique. His mother had invited her to the party tomorrow, and he had completely forgotten to message her and suggest as politely as he could that she not show up.

Email was risky, now that it was so close. He would have to text her. Even though that seemed a little too familiar, it was the only way to ensure she got his note.

He kicked his shoes off and shut the door with his elbow as he pulled out his phone. Best to keep the message simple and short.

Mom didn't realize we had split.

Don't feel obligated to attend the party.

There. That wouldn't be insulting, but it would also make clear that his mother had invited her, and not him. The last thing he needed was for Angelique to believe that something about his situation had changed.

No dots appeared to signal that she was responding, so he set his phone on the table and headed to his bedroom. Lorelei definitely had him dressing more casually. He even kept a pair of jeans and a T-shirt in his office now. He had to laugh. This was bound to be a good thing.

By the time he pulled up in front of Linda's house, he was starving. He knocked on the exterior door, but Linda, not Lorelei, opened it.

She didn't seem particularly pleased to see him. With her sour expression and tight hair bun, she looked like the old lady in that painting, the one standing by a man holding a pitchfork. *American Gothic*.

"Oh, it's you," Linda said. "You haven't wised up yet."

"I'm sorry?"

"That girl is nothing but trouble. She's never going to grow up."

"I'm under the impression that most people take life a little too seriously," Micah said. "Maybe we should be more like Lorelei."

As the woman stared him down, he spotted Lorelei at the top of the stairs. She wore a pale blue skirt and a white sweater, looking as lovely as a spring sky.

"Are you trying to warn Micah away from me?" Lorelei said. "I know you'd rather have him for yourself, but at least let me have little time to date him before he throws me over for you."

She reached the bottom step and kissed the old lady on the cheek before taking Micah's hand. "Just let me down easy when it's time," she said to Micah.

Linda shook her head at the both of them as they hurried down the walk to his car.

"I don't think she likes you," Micah said.

"Nonsense. She adores me. She's just mad right now, because she told my mother about the lease and the entire quilting circle threatened to kick her out unless she revoked it."

They settled in his car. "Does that mean you don't have to sign it?"

"Apparently not."

"Excellent." He started the car. "One problem solved."

"Thank goodness."

He broached the next subject carefully. "So, my parents gave me a gift card to this restaurant I really like in Branson. I thought we could use it for dinner."

Lorelei's eyebrows lifted in suspicion. "Micah Livingston, are you trying to find a way to avoid going to McDonald's for your birthday dinner, since that's all I can afford?"

He laughed. There was no pulling one over on her. "Maybe."

She settled back in her seat. "I'll allow it. And you don't have to pretend about the gift card either."

"I did get a card," he said. "But okay."

They spent the next couple of hours in easy

companionship. Micah felt like he hadn't smiled this much in years. Maybe not ever.

After dinner, they held hands and strolled along the shore of Table Rock Lake. The lights of the city reflected on the water, and people walked in every direction, a sharp contrast with the opposite shore and Applebottom's quiet community.

"I like it over here," Lorelei said. "But I admit, I prefer to live in the quiet and visit the crazy, rather than the other way around."

"Funny, I was just thinking about that. How the two sides of the lake have such different feels."

"It's because all the tourists are over here. In Applebottom, you can't walk three steps without seeing someone who changed your diaper."

Micah laughed. "That's a horrible thought."

"I know. I'm terrible."

Micah stopped and gathered her in his arms. "No. You're perfect."

They stood there, strangers streaming past them along the busy boardwalk full of businesses, parking lots, and theaters. But what mattered most was that they knew each other, and they knew where they came from. And whether they were surrounded by no one important, or everyone they knew, Micah felt in that moment, that they were meant to be.

CHAPTER 17

The last thing Lorelei's sister said to her before they parted, having worked for two hours on Lorelei's makeup, hair, and outfit for Micah's birthday party, was, "Don't let them get you down."

But as Lorelei drove up to the lake house, realizing that her ancient backfiring Civic was about to be handled by a valet, she wasn't sure she could do it.

The circle drive was lined with all manner of fancy cars. Maserati. Mercedes. Infinity. Lexus. There were sports cars she couldn't even identify.

She felt faint as she chugged up to the front. To his credit, the valet did not so much as blink an eye as he opened her door to let her out. "Thank you," he said as he sat in her seat.

"Sometimes she stumbles a little when you turn her off," Lorelei said quickly. "And if you can't get her started, just come get me. I know exactly how to push the gas and rev it to make sure she keeps going."

He nodded. "Will do, Miss Spencer."

He knew her name. Did they all memorize something? She was quite sure she never seen him before. The company logo on his shirt was not one from Applebottom.

Weird.

Another couple stepped out of a car behind hers and a second valet rushed to take their car. As the first man drove off in her Civic, Lorelei steeled herself. Maybe she should walk in with these other people to avoid having to show up completely alone. She wished she'd dragged her sister with her. Or Bethany. Heck, she'd even take grumpy Candace right now.

The other couple moved along the walk, and Lorelei hurried to catch up to them. They held a large package wrapped in silver.

Lorelei had given Micah his present last night. The date had been magical, and he'd seemed genuinely appreciative of the intricate rope bracelet she'd woven for him.

But this was not the same. Her stress levels were maxing out.

The other couple hadn't noticed she was following them. The woman wore a silver gown and fancy heels with red soles.

Lorelei tugged at her dress. She had borrowed it

from her sister, who had worn it several years before to some college formal. It was shimmery and red, with a square neckline.

Other than the color, it seemed elegant and subdued. She hadn't owned any tall red heels, and Mandy's shoes didn't fit her. A pair of simple black pumps was the best she could do.

She felt so outclassed.

She gripped her small clutch as the other couple knocked on the door. A tall solemn-faced man in a black shirt and pants opened it.

"Welcome, Mr. and Mrs. Washington," he said to the couple in front of her. "Feel free to leave your gift on the table by the entry." He pointed into the foyer.

He caught sight of Lorelei. "Miss Spencer," he said. "The young Mr. Livingston asked me to escort you directly to him as soon as you arrived."

The couple turned to look at her in surprise. She knew none of these people, or why any of them knew her name, and she felt her nerves rattling around in her brain like loose change.

But she was grateful that she was going directly to Micah. He was literally the only person she felt comfortable with—other than maybe Maya and Chief.

The man extended his arm, and Lorelei took it. He escorted her in the opposite direction than she had gone a few nights before, away from the study, and into a long elegant living room.

At the far end, a man in a tux played the piano. A woman in a long, sparkly gold gown stood next to the baby grand, singing a soulful rendition of "I'll Close My Eyes."

Micah sat in an oversized armchair, like a king holding court on a throne. Quite a number of people had dragged smaller chairs to sit near him. Lorelei didn't know any of them. She was pretty sure none of them were from Applebottom.

Which seemed a little strange. Micah had gone to high school here. Surely they'd invited some of his old friends.

This crew all seemed about his age, and were dressed gorgeously in suits and dresses she could only guess were from fancy boutiques she'd never been in and probably never would. It looked like a magazine photo come to life.

Her step faltered just a few steps past the door, and the man who held her arm paused to look at her. "Everything okay?" he asked.

"You knew my name," Lorelei said quickly. "Do you know theirs?"

"Why, certainly. That's Mr. George Stone and Mr. Mark Halliday, both from young Mr. Livingston's law school. Then Miss Adriana Cartier and Miss Melanie Hall, who arrived with the two gentlemen."

"Who is the girl in white?" Lorelei asked.

This one sat the closest to Micah, and she looked like a freaking angel. Her white dress shimmered from the narrow straps on her shoulders all the way to the floor. Her hair was soft gold, falling in movie star waves down her back. The way she looked at Micah was startlingly familiar, as if she possessed some particular hold on him that everyone should know about.

"That is Angelique Martin. Also from the law school."

So this was the one Micah's mother had talked about. Angelique was definitely an ex. Great. That beautiful, and a lawyer too.

Once again, Lorelei wanted the tiles to split apart and take her into some deep dark cavern where she could curl up into a ball.

But this was her moment. She could cower, or she could stand tall.

Lorelei moved forward, and the man walked with her. She let go of him just as they got close enough for the others to notice her.

"Lorelei," Micah said, rising from his chair. "You made it."

"Of course." She made eye contact with each person sitting nearby. This was her only salvo, so she let it loose. "George, Mark, Adriana, Melanie, I'm so glad you could come to Micah's birthday." She turned to Angelique. "And Angelique. I'm a little surprised to see you here, but you look lovely."

Lorelei slid her arm through Micah's. "I hope you don't mind that I'm stealing my birthday boy."

No one spoke. They seemed a little in shock.

She gave them a nod and led Micah away.

"You're full of surprises," he said.

Lorelei's heart was pounding so hard that she could scarcely hear him. "Please don't be mad."

Micah stopped. "Mad? I thought was brilliant. That was the most amazing display of self-assurance I've seen tonight."

Lorelei shoulders relaxed. "Really? Because I was terrified."

"You saved me. It was brilliant." He picked up her hand and kissed her fingers. "Let's go find something to eat. Maya promised she would make some real food, in addition to the silly hors d'oeuvres that my parents are serving."

They hurried to the kitchen, where a whole collection of uniformed catering employees were briskly loading trays.

Maya stood near the door, holding Chief in her arms. Her face broke out in a smile when she saw Micah. "There you are," she said. "Look at these people taking over my kitchen."

"Hello, Maya," Lorelei said. "How is Chief holding up with all the activity?"

"He is shaking like a leaf," she said.

Lorelei petted the little dog's head. "Poor thing."

"Just point me in the direction of some real food, and you and Chief can escape," Micah said. "No sense torturing the poor guy."

"I'll fetch it for you," she said. She headed over to the fridge, sidestepping the caterers and their big silver trays. She rummaged for a moment and returned with a small container filled with cocktail wieners wrapped in baked croissants. Lorelei recognized them immediately, because she had made pigs in a blanket a million times with her sister.

"Let me heat them." Maya forged through the crowd again.

Micah grinned at Lorelei. "This party is already better than my parents' usual ones."

Lorelei held on to his arm, her anxiety starting to ebb. This was fine. Maybe she could even have fun.

Maya returned and passed him the container. "Enjoy them."

"Perfect," Micah said. He showed them to Lorelei. "Want one? I will only share with you."

"Lucky me," Lorelei said, pulling one of the warm croissants out of the box.

"You crazy lovebirds." Maya stood on her tiptoes to kiss his cheek. "Happy birthday, sweet boy."

Lorelei and Micah hid near the pantry eating his pigs in a blanket, and quietly made fun of the fancy food on all the trays.

"I don't even know what that black stuff is," Lorelei said. "Is it caviar?"

"Fish eggs," Micah said. "It doesn't deserve a fancy name like caviar. It's salty and disgusting."

Lorelei laughed. "Thank goodness Maya got you something good."

"It's my party, I'll eat pork parts if I want to."

Suddenly, the air seemed supercharged. The caterers all worked more stiffly, and the noise quieted to the point that they could hear the singer again in the other room.

Lorelei turned to see Micah's mother standing at the door to the kitchen. She drifted toward them in a long black gown with lace sleeves.

"Micah, darling, you're missing your own party."

Micah lifted the container. "I've got my party right here."

Alicia frowned at the contents, then took the plastic tub from his hands and set it on the counter. "Hopefully you're done with those, because we should really go greet some of the guests. Particularly the law partners from Springfield. It seems that there could be an opening for a junior partner, and given that it's only an hour away, you could still manage some of the caseload here in Applebottom, while also reaping the benefit of becoming part of a larger firm."

Lorelei felt her heart thud again. What was this?

"Really?" Micah said. "Whose firm?"

Now Alicia smiled. "Lockingham and Madison," she said.

"Well, okay," Micah said. "Might as well aim for the sky. Let's go."

He seemed to have forgotten her. As Micah and his

mother headed out of the kitchen, Lorelei followed at a slower pace. Was she supposed to go with him? Should she busy herself while they had this business meeting?

Unfortunately, Micah didn't think to turn and give her any clue.

They turned down a small hall and into completely different style of room. There was no piano in here, but multiple small tables with round leather chairs. The room was filled mostly with men in suits, although a few of them had women standing near them or sitting close by. Periodically a round of uproarious laughter would fill the room.

Lorelei felt completely out of place. No one in here was under the age of fifty, other than Micah. She stopped at the door.

"Micah," a large man called out, extending his hand as he headed toward him. "So glad you could finally join your party."

Micah was immediately surrounded by other men, all wishing him happy birthday and shaking his hand.

Lorelei stood in the doorway, unsure what to do.

After a few greetings, Alicia turned around and spotted her. "You can run along," she said, towering over Lorelei in another pair of impossible heels. "Micah has important things to discuss."

Then she literally closed the door in Lorelei's face.

This was the worst. Lorelei took two steps back,

fighting off tears. What was she supposed to do? Sit somewhere and wait? Leave?

All of a sudden everything she felt seemed inconsequential. Micah might become a partner of a firm in Springfield. *Aim for the sky*, he'd said.

And he'd been in a relationship with that angel goddess in the other room. Obviously, she was angling to get him back.

How in the world could someone like Lorelei hang on to someone like Micah when they'd really only had three dates and had barely done more than kiss?

This was too much. It was too soon, and this could not work. It didn't matter how heartfelt their time had been. Or how happy they seemed. This was life.

Just like Gary. Like college.

She couldn't even burn some paper without it turning into a disaster.

Lorelei turned and hurried back to the main foyer. She'd almost made it to the door when a swish of white got her attention.

It was Angelique. Of course it was.

"I don't think I quite caught your name," she said. "Have we met?"

Lorelei wanted to throw up. "I just heard about you, is all." She couldn't even look up, her gaze stuck on the woman's gleaming white shoes.

"I'm guessing you're the reason Micah not-so-subtly suggested I should avoid his party."

He did that? Lorelei stood a little straighter. "I think there was a little misunderstanding with his mom," she said.

"Oh, there was no misunderstanding," Angelique said. "Alicia wanted me here. She feels that Micah has gotten too comfortable in this little community, and he needs to return to his real career. The direction he was *supposed* to take."

"I see." Lorelei shrank down again.

"But it was really nice to meet you," Angelique said. "Whatever your name is." She turned and headed back toward the room with the piano.

Lorelei stood there for a moment, trying to think. What should she do? Obviously, everyone had a plan for Micah. And Micah was so eager to go talk to them about it that he'd forgotten about her.

She didn't fit in here. It didn't matter whether it happened today, or next month, or even a year from now. Lorelei was never going to fit in Micah's world.

She had plans of her own. College. A degree. She was already forcing a separation between them.

What made the most sense at that moment, and probably forever, was for Lorelei to cut her losses and get the heck out.

CHAPTER 18

For the next several days, Lorelei left her phone with her sister. She also stayed in Mandy's spare bedroom, which was only just now transitioning into a nursery for the new baby.

It was sort of soothing, spending her days painting the walls a relaxing mint green, hanging curtains, and laughing over her ineptitude in setting up a swing. Her heart healed a little, and her thoughts became clearer.

She called over to the University and discovered that late registration was still available for her for two more weeks, and the counselor said she would approve Lorelei to sign up for her final courses, despite the skipped semester.

It turned out she had passed all her classes last fall, having forgotten that some of the professors would drop her lowest grade. So, as long as she took a full load, she would be able to graduate in December.

She currently didn't have a dorm, but housing assured her that, as a senior, she'd be at the top of the waitlist, and rooms always opened up at the last minute.

So that was done.

Lorelei didn't know if Micah had written her or not. She'd asked Mandy to avoid telling her about any of her calls or messages unless they were from Bethany or Candace.

If Micah said something to her that needed a response, Lorelei simply trusted her sister to handle it.

Because of this, she had no indication of how Micah might be handling their separation until her grandma came over to bring a box of sandwiches and teacakes on Thursday night.

Lorelei held three-year-old Shila in her lap as Mandy eagerly watched Grandma Betty unpack the boxes of delicate frosted cakes and filled sandwiches.

"Me me me me," Shila called, reaching her stubby fingers toward the frosting. "I like cake."

"Aunty Lor-Lor will let you have all the teacakes you want," Lorelei said.

"Only after she's had a few sandwiches," Mandy added.

"And then Great Grandma Betty will give you even more cake," her grandmother said.

Mandy shook her head. "Spoiled. Totally spoiled."

"As it should be." Grandma Betty turned to Lorelei. "So, are you ghosting Micah?"

The two sisters looked at her, shocked.

"Who told you what ghosting meant?" Lorelei asked.

Grandma Betty shrugged. "I pick up a thing or two on the Facepage."

Mandy busted out laughing. "I think you mean Facebook, Grandma."

Betty waved the comment away. "It doesn't matter. Micah has shown up to my tea shop three times this week."

Mandy plucked a pimento sandwich from the box. "Has he asked after Lorelei?"

Grandma Betty took out two more and put them on Mandy's plate. "Only every time he's walked in the door."

Lorelei was glad she had Shila in her lap to focus on. She passed the little girl a bite of bread.

Mandy pushed a napkin closer to Shila. "Well, it doesn't matter. In a couple weeks, Lorelei is packing up and heading back to the University."

"I'm so glad it's worked out," Grandma said. "That's the best news I've heard today." She picked up a perfectly frosted round pink cake and passed it to Lorelei. "Extra cake for you!"

No one brought up Micah again, but Lorelei felt riddled with guilt. She should at least tell him goodbye or something. She wondered if he had already taken the position in Springfield—and, if so, when it might start.

None of these were questions she deserved the answer to. She'd walked out on a future with Micah last weekend, at his birthday party no less. It was better if they both moved on with a clean break.

Lorelei didn't actually collect her phone from her sister until moving day. It turned out that using the landline for her girlfriends, and seeing people in person, was actually a better way to communicate.

As her father arranged and rearranged her trunk and backseat to fit all her things, Lorelei powered up the freshly charged phone, knowing she would have no time to obsess over any messages Micah had left.

But her sister came up beside her and said, "I deleted all of his texts."

Lorelei glanced up from the phone. Mandy seemed tired, her hands resting on her growing belly. The baby would be born while Lorelei was away, but she would drive back to meet him. "And you're sure that was the best for me?"

"Absolutely sure," Mandy said. "Mostly he was just asking if you were okay."

"Did you ever tell him anything?"

"Just that I had your phone and good luck with his decisions." She bent over to give Lorelei a hug. Lorelei held on to this moment, realizing that it could be more precious than she realized. The next time she came, her family would have another member.

Family was the most solid thing in your life, and yet completely ephemeral. Every year, new ones could arrive, and cherished ones could be lost, just as Micah lost Josh.

The lump in her throat as she hugged her family goodbye was so great that she had trouble speaking her farewells.

But eventually she started her little car, which purred since her father had paid to have the engine overhauled. She headed south to Fayetteville, where she would finish her degree in English, take a few business courses, and figure out what was next.

Micah had been a lovely diversion, and definitely served his purpose in erasing Gary from her mind. But it hadn't worked out. Life moved on.

CHAPTER 19

*M*icah turned in his oversized office chair. His dad had been coming into the office most days since his return, and while the room was spacious and had plenty of seating, it felt crowded when both of them were trying to work.

He flipped through the packet of papers in his hand once more. It was the confidentiality agreement that he would sign with Lockingham and Madison as he went into the final interviews with the partners.

It was all just a formality. The position was his if he wanted it. He would bring with him enough cases to justify coming aboard, and the way the firm was growing, he would have plenty more handed to him when he got there.

Still, he hesitated.

He liked his life in Applebottom. It was more comfortable than he had expected.

Seeing his law school friends at his birthday party had shown him that his old lifestyle was not what he wanted it all. It was pretentious and false, and full of pressures for all the wrong reasons.

Angelique had already known about the offer in Springfield somehow, and had not-so-subtly suggested that she was willing to move there. Springfield had many prestigious firms, she said, and wouldn't it be fun if down the line they opened a practice together?

That seemed to be about the worst idea of all. Something about Angelique rubbed him wrong now. She was an elitist and a snob. How had ever thought he wanted someone like her as a wife?

The real reason for his party had become clear. His parents seemed determined to set him on the path he had deliberately walked away from several years before.

He startled when his father spoke. "Something wrong with the agreement?"

"No, it's all pretty standard stuff."

"Is it still about that girl?"

Micah shrugged. "I heard she left yesterday for University. She still has a semester left."

"Five months isn't that long," he said.

"Probably not." Micah didn't really want to explain it all.

His dad stood up. "That's about as many hours as I want to put in. I think your mother and I are going to head to New York for a few days. You have every-thing handled around here?"

Micah sat back in his chair. They were already leaving again? His dad had acted as though he was about ready to take over the firm. "Should I delay Springfield?"

"No, no, no. It will be fine. I'll be back."

But Micah wondered. His father hadn't been able to put in a whole day once since he'd returned to the office. The caseload here was solid. Even if Micah took some of the more far-flung cases with him to Springfield, his dad would have more work from Applebottom clients than he could complete in a couple hours a day. Court alone was two days a week.

Still, all Micah said was, "Have a good time."

His father took his jacket from the rack and slid it on. He greeted Marianne as he walked out, and then Micah was left to his office again.

Marianne moved to the doorway. "You still have your eleven o'clock," she said. "The mayor."

"Right," Micah said. "It's fine."

Marianne hesitated, as if she wanted to say some-thing about his father, but then she turned and went back to her desk.

Maybe Micah could hire an actual legal assistant to help. Not that one would be easy to lure to Apple-bottom. No one with the right credentials lived in town. He could send out feelers to some of the nearby schools. He glanced down at the Springfield agreement again. Despite what his father had said, he was definitely going to have to delay that decision.

He brought out the file for T-bone, Applebottom's rather unusual mayor. Micah had been sworn to secrecy on this matter, even though he had already assured T-bone that as part of the attorney-client privilege, he was not at liberty to divulge anything that was said between them.

But it was interesting for sure. T-bone wanted a will. That in itself wasn't unusual. T-bone owned an RV Park just outside of town, and as a single man with no family, he should be thinking about where his property would go upon his death.

The strange part was that a young man had showed up in town claiming to be T-bone's son. Micah had requested birth and legal records pertaining to the boy, and was prepared to subtly arrange for a DNA test should T-bone request it.

The birth certificate that had arrived from Seattle listed T-bone's legal name as the father. This, of course, didn't mean that much. A woman could put down anybody on that paperwork.

Micah smiled as he reviewed T-bone's full legal name. He might be the only person in Applebottom who knew it.

His phone buzzed.

"The mayor is here," Marianne said.

"Send him on back."

Micah stood as T-bone lumbered through the door. He wore his usual outfit, a T-shirt with a black leather motorcycle vest, jeans laden with silver chains, and heavy black boots. His scraggly hair was tied back for the occasion, and he stroked the length of his wiry beard as if he was anxious.

Behind him was a rather good-looking young man of twenty-five. And when they stood side-by-side, both with their legs spread the same width apart, one arm behind their backs and one at their sides, identical eyes looking at him, Micah knew there would be no need for a DNA test.

This was definitely T-bone's son.

"Sit down," he said, gesturing to the sofa. "We can go over all this."

When they were settled, T-bone said, "I got the shock of my life when Luke here showed up at the RV Park."

"He wasn't easy to find," Luke said. He explained that his mother had recently died, and only going through her papers had he learned about his biological father.

"You never knew?" Micah asked.

"I learned T-bone's name when I got my driver's license at sixteen," Luke said. "I was kind of an angry kid, though, so I took off and never bothered looking anybody up."

"What changed your mind?"

"Right before she died, Mom gave me bunch of

pictures of her and T-bone. Some letters. She told me if I wanted to find my dad, here he was."

Micah turned to T-bone. "She didn't tell you she was pregnant?"

"No, sir," T-bone said. "She ran off with some other guy. I never heard from her again till Luke here walked in my door."

"Can I see some of those letters?" Micah asked.

Luke passed the box over. Micah scanned through them quickly. It seemed as though the woman had written a lot of notes to T-bone that she never sent. She knew she'd made a mistake in leaving with this other man. She was pregnant.

There was a lot of self-loathing in the letters. Micah's heart panged.

"I would've stepped up," T-bone said. "If I need to resign as mayor over this, I will. But I promise you, I would've stepped up."

Micah waved off T-bone's concern. "I think this is fine. If anything, Applebottom is going to be delighted to find out that you have a son. They don't need the details. The birth certificate with your name is in order. The timeline of pregnancy and when you last saw each other is all well and good." He met T-bone's gaze. "Do you want a DNA test?"

"Naw," T-bone said. "Look at the boy. He's like me all over again."

Micah passed Luke the box. "I completely agree. I saw the resemblance immediately."

"So did I," Luke said.

Micah sat back. "So what do you want out of this relationship, Luke? Are you going to hang around? Do you have a life somewhere?"

"I've been working as a mechanic in Montana," Luke said. "But I've been going to vet school on the side. It's just expensive, so I've had to take my time. I got a little sidetracked with mom dying." He glanced over at T-bone. "I did go help her. She wasn't alone."

T-bone nodded, his gaze down at his clasped hands.

"Are you thinking of something around here?" Micah asked.

"Thinkin' about it," Luke said. "T-bone said there was lots of need for a mechanic. People've been towing their cars to Branson. There's a decent vet school over at Fisher College just forty-five minutes away. I haven't looked into transferring my credits or anything yet, but I think it could work."

Micah liked this young man. He seemed very forthright. Nothing about him set off any internal scam alerts.

"I'll go ahead and draw up this will, T-bone, with the addition of an heir. Everything looks good on my end, and if you need help from me in any way in presenting the situation to town, I'll be happy to speak on your behalf."

"I think I can handle it," T-bone said. "As long as

you're sure it's okay for me to keep serving as mayor."

"You know as well as I do that nobody else wants to be mayor," Micah said. "I wouldn't worry about it in the least."

T-bone shifted like he was about to stand up, but then he settled in again. "There's a rumor going about that you might be headin' to Springfield," he said.

"Just a rumor," Micah said. "Dad's leaving for New York, and I'm going to be needed here for a while."

T-bone nodded. "That's good. I thought maybe Miss Lorelei takin' off like she did might've done you in for Applebottom."

Micah could always count on T-bone to call it like he saw it.

"I'm fine," Micah assured him, even though he wasn't entirely sure he was.

"I just know if I could do it all over again," T-bone went on, "I would move mountains to make sure she knew how I felt."

Luke nodded grimly.

Both of the men had their heads bowed. T-bone had lost twenty-five years with his son because he let this woman go. That was just the way love went. Broken hearts strewn everywhere.

As for him, he and Lorelei had barely gotten started. What, three dates? Four if you counted the party?

But maybe that didn't matter. They'd known each other. They grew up in the same place. That meant they had a history that outsiders could never understand.

Certainly not Angelique. She'd never even met his brother Josh before he died. Lorelei had.

But what could he do about it? Lorelei had left for Fayetteville.

"Noted," he said. "I'll take it under advisement."

And with that, the three men stood up and shook hands.

Now all that was left was the paperwork and collecting the scattered pieces of the *what ifs* and *if onlys*.

CHAPTER 20

*L*orelei was sitting in her small business administration class when she got the text.

Headed to the hospital. Baby Thomas is on his way.

She jumped from her seat, then sat down again as fifty heads all turned her direction.

"Sorry," she murmured.

There were only ten minutes left in the lecture. She could wait that long.

Thankfully, this was her last class for the day, and tomorrow she had nothing but a lab for her literature workshop. Lorelei could email the teaching assistant and let her know she would make it up when she got back.

She was about to get a nephew!

The moment her class was dismissed, she fired a quick message back to her sister saying she would be there in a few hours, and rushed to her dorm to pack some clothes.

Thomas was arriving a few days before his due date, but that was perfect. Next week was Thanksgiving, which meant Lorelei could get an early start on the holiday and she would have a precious eleven whole days at home with the new baby before she had to be back.

By the time she arrived at the hospital in Branson, her entire family had assembled in the waiting room of the maternity wing. Her mother was inside with Mandy, but her father, Uncle Sam, Grandma Betty, Grandmother and Grandpap Humphries had already assembled.

"George's family is on the way," her father said, referring to Mandy's husband. "It's five hours for them."

"She couldn't have given us more warning?" Lorelei asked, plunking into a seat beside her dad.

"She didn't quite believe it when she woke up with the contractions," Grandma Betty said. "Although I told her that this baby was going to be early. He already dropped."

"It won't be long now," Grandmother Etta said. She was knitting a mint green blanket to match the nursery. "She's been pushing for a spell."

Poor Mandy. Her sister had told her that they hadn't given her the drugs near fast enough with Shila, and it felt like her insides were on strike.

"Where's Shila?" Lorelei asked.

"She's in there with them," Grandma Betty said. "Mandy said it helped keep her calm to see her little girl, proof that she could survive this thing."

Grandmother Etta rolled her eyes. "Nothing more natural than having a baby."

They were all wrong about how long it was going to take. George's family arrived, and there was still an hour to spare before George finally came to the waiting room to say that Thomas had arrived safely. He would be rolling to the nursery to be cleaned up in about ten minutes.

All the grandmothers instantly burst into tears. The men stood to shake George's hand.

Lorelei slipped down the hall to check on her sister.

Mandy lay back in the bed, all tucked in, the baby in her arms. Their mother adjusted her pillows.

Shila sat on a chair in the corner, licking a lollipop. She looked up at Lorelei. "Baby brother," she said, then resumed eating the candy.

Lorelei walked up to her sister and gazed down at the baby. Only his little face was visible beneath the tiny striped hat and the bundle of the blanket.

"Hello, my little nephew," Lorelei said. "I'm glad to finally meet you."

"Glad you made it," Mandy said, exhaustion in her voice. "This was a long one."

Lorelei nodded. "Four hours longer than Shila."

A nurse rolled up a plastic baby bed. "Time for little Thomas to go get cleaned up," she said. "We'll be right back."

"Please wait for George before you take him," Mandy said. "I hate it when the baby leaves the room."

"I'll go with the baby until George catches up," Lorelei said. "Everyone's congratulating him like he did all the pushing."

Mandy let out a little chuckle, then grimaced, pressing her hand to her belly. "Don't make me laugh. But okay."

The nurse placed the baby in the plastic bassinet, and Lorelei puffed with importance that she got to escort the baby down to the nursery. Several people in the halls paused to admire him as they passed the other rooms.

George caught up with her partway. "I can take over," he said.

Lorelei leaned down to touch the baby's head as they walked along. "See you soon," she said.

The next couple days were long. Lorelei and her mother and the two grandmothers took turns helping out Mandy. Lorelei no longer had her apartment at Linda's to escape to, so she bounced between

Betty's house, her parents', and occasionally slept on the sofa at Mandy's.

On the Monday before Thanksgiving, Lorelei was eating oatmeal at her parents' house when her dad suddenly jumped out of his chair. He walked over to the basket near the door where they kept all the bills.

"I completely forgot with the baby and all," he said. He dug through the basket and pulled out an envelope. "You got something from the judge."

Lorelei accepted the long envelope. What was this?

She slid the flap open. It was a reminder that she only had thirty more days to complete her community service or her she would have to reappear in court.

"Oh, no," she said.

"Everything okay?" her dad asked. "I'm sorry I didn't give it to you sooner."

"No, it's fine. I just have to do the community service in thirty days and I'm only going to be here this week. I won't be back in time to do it before finals."

"Is there something you can do while you're here now? Maybe serve Thanksgiving dinner at one of the soup kitchens?"

Now that was an idea. "I'll call over to the court and ask," Lorelei said. "I have no idea where that list of approved community service went."

"There's a dinner down at the Methodist Church,"

her dad said. "And if they'll let you do it in Branson, I'm sure there's quite a few."

Lorelei got the dinner approved as her community service and ended up driving up to the Methodist Church early in the morning on Thanksgiving day. She had to get there for the first wave in order to make sure she got her eight hours in. She wiped her bleary eyes, tied her hair back, and dove in.

She knew most of the women who were helping out. Some were former teachers. Others owned little shops about town. Normally Betty would be there, too, but this year she was cooking dinner for both families, who had decided to remain in town for the holiday and spend more time with baby Thomas.

The hours passed quickly as she crumbled bread for stuffing and stirred great vats of chicken broth. As serving time approached, Gertrude and Maude arrived with a car full of pies.

Maude tugged off her gloves, her tight black-and-silver curls spilling from her knit hat. "Lorelei," she said, "you be a dear and help us bring in these pies."

"Of course," Lorelei said. "Good morning, Gertrude."

Gertrude, looking as sour and weathered as always, grunted a greeting.

Lorelei knew the two ladies well. They had owned the Applebottom Pie Shoppe since before she was born, and they regularly got embroiled in feuds with Grandma Betty over whose desserts were more appropriate for which holiday.

She headed out into the cold, late afternoon air and waited while Gertrude opened the back.

Gertrude had always intrigued Lorelei. She was a contemporary to Grandma Betty, and the two of them had gone to school together. But while Betty had married, had a daughter, and grandchildren, Gertrude had remained single.

Gertrude was an only daughter of an only son. Her father had not run the pie shop that her grandfather built, leaving Gertrude in charge in her early twenties at his death. Gertrude had run the shop somewhat successfully until about thirty years ago, when the recession hit Branson hard, which trickled down to Applebottom. This made owning a shop that only sold pies close to impossible.

By then, Gertrude's mother had passed, and her father was in the Applebottom Nursing Home. Gertrude had struggled mightily to keep the shop going.

Lorelei hadn't been around then, and she only knew the story from what her grandmother had hinted at throughout the years. Maybe that failure to succeed had caused Gertrude to be so sour. Her partner Maude had swooped in to invest for half ownership. They kept the business afloat until the economy recovered.

Now the two of them, tall slender gray-haired

irascible Gertrude and plump, grandmotherly, sweet-natured Maude, stood as two strong pillars in the community.

Gertrude noticed Lorelei's scrutiny as they arranged pies on a silver cart. "I see you trying to figure out how I tick," she snapped. "Just because you have problems, doesn't mean you can pin any on me."

Lorelei was taken aback. "Why would I pin any of my problems on you?"

Gertrude slammed the trunk lid shut. "Why do you think you're doing community service? You got six people to blame as to why Judge Hughes called you in when Fred was going to let your little afternoon bonfire go unpunished."

Really? Interesting.

"Was my grandmother in on this?" Lorelei asked.

Gertrude gave the cart a hefty shove to make it move over the uneven surface of the parking lot. "That woman was the start of it all. I said you could take care of yourself. They had to go meddle. And now you're spending a perfectly good Thanksgiving up here with a bunch of old women."

"I don't mind," Lorelei said. She walked ahead of Gertrude and the cart, ready to help steer if it veered off course. "Mandy's house is crowded with people, anyway. I'll be back in time for their dinner."

Maude waited just inside the door and motioned them inside. "Come on in out of the cold. And I don't mean the weather. The frost coming off Gertrude could freeze a bull."

Gertrude *harrumphed* as she rolled the cart to the desert table. The three of them unpacked the boxes, cutting pieces to set on plates for easy pickup.

Another group of volunteers began setting the tables with pretty tablecloths and candles. It was a right nice meal they were preparing. Lorelei wished she'd known to volunteer at it before.

She stacked the empty pie tins to carry to the back. She'd almost made it to the door to the kitchen when she stopped cold at the sound of the familiar voice.

"Everything smells so good."

Micah.

What was he doing here?

Lorelei's first thought was that the town had once again intervened to put them together. She flashed hot with anger and annoyance.

But then Doris, who headed up the serving committee, said to him, "I love how you come in to serve every year," she said. "It does my heart good to see young men like you in here volunteering."

Micah served the Thanksgiving meal every year?

"Should I take my usual position?" he asked.

"Absolutely. Everyone expects the town lawyer to serve up the turkey."

When Micah walked through the door from the kitchen to the main hall, Lorelei's heart leapt into her throat. He wore a soft blue sweater and dark gray pants, all covered with a crisp white apron. He held two sets of serving tongs.

His beard was back, just like when they were first together. He looked so professional and dapper, she felt regret all the way to her toes.

When he saw her, he also went still.

A few of the aluminum pie tins crumpled in her tight grip. "Micah. I didn't know you would be here."

"Is this your community service?"

She nodded. "I was running out of time and had to do something before I went back to school."

His face spread into a slow grin, and her stomach got all quivery. Her body tingled with competing emotions. Joy at seeing him. Regret that they'd parted badly. Relief that he would smile at her.

They stood there for a moment just looking at each other, and Maude gently took the stack of pie tins from Lorelei. "You go serve the dressing," she said.

"Here's your spot," Doris said to Micah, setting down a deep tray stacked with turkey. "Lorelei, sounds like you're here."

The steaming container of stuffing sat directly next to the turkey. They'd be serving side-by-side.

She had no time to think on it. The doors to the hall were opened from the foyer and the first trickle of people came through, mostly individual men in ragged coats. Micah greeted each one cordially and offered them white or dark meat. They developed a rhythm as more people began to stream in, families, often women with children. Elderly, sometimes alone, others with a caregiver or a spouse.

Lorelei's eyes teared up multiple times as children gratefully held up their plates for seconds. She tried to imagine her niece or nephew not having enough to eat, and struggled not to break down even as she fed these children she'd never met.

When they finally reached their first lull, she asked Micah, "I had no idea so many people were hungry in Applebottom. I've never seen a homeless person in town."

"There's a lot of squatters in the woods and up in the mountains," Micah said. "People who, for whatever reason, want to stay away from the public eye."

"How do they get food and clothes?"

"We have food banks. Some of the churches serve meals once or twice a week. We have spots where we leave clothing, blankets, and toiletries for them to find."

Lorelei felt her eyes opened in a way she had never known before. "Is it enough? Some of these people don't seem as though they get enough to eat."

"It's never enough," Micah said. "All we can do is stay the course and keep helping where we can."

"Have you always done this? How do you know so much?"

He smiled at a latecomer and served him a

generous helping of turkey. She added a scoop of dressing and passed over his plate.

"After Josh died," Micah said, "I started doing more helpful things. My family has way more than we need. It made sense for me to give back as much as I could."

How could she not have been aware of this? What else was there about Micah she didn't know?

"I love that," she said. "I wish I had more, so that I could give more. I'm perpetually broke."

"You're here," he said. "It's a start."

By a judge's order, Lorelei thought. That hardly counted for anything.

"Is your family in town?" she asked. "Are you ditching them for this?"

He shook his head. "My family is never in town for Thanksgiving anymore. Christmas, either. Holidays are … hard."

"Where are they?"

"Milan, this year."

"You don't go?"

"I tried. But it doesn't feel right either. I'd rather be here, doing this."

But this would be over soon. And Micah would be alone.

"I have to stay here through cleanup to get my eight hours," Lorelei said in a rush. "So my family is holding Thanksgiving dinner for me. Would you like to come?"

"Oh, I wouldn't want to intrude on your family gathering," he said. "Traditionally I go for a run after eating here."

"But I really want you to come," she said.

"Are you sure?"

"I am."

They paused to serve another family—a man, woman, and a little girl not much bigger than Shila.

"Okay," Micah said when the line was clear. "I might as well stay here with you and clean up."

Lorelei's heart leapt. Yes, this was the right thing. Serving the dinner, and leaving with Micah. She could think of no more perfect way to spend her day.

CHAPTER 21

Micah waited for Lorelei to park before getting out of his own car. How had this happened exactly? Instead of a day of watching football and getting a few miles in, he was right back in the belly of the whale with Lorelei, and her family to boot.

She would leave again this weekend, and he'd have to start the process of disengaging from his hope again.

But maybe this day would be worth it.

He caught up to her on the sidewalk. "Is this your sister's house?"

"Yeah," she said. "We all felt it would be easier on Mandy to be in her own space since Thomas just arrived a week ago. It'll be crowded though."

"I don't think I've seen a baby that small in years."

"He doesn't do a lot!"

Lorelei opened the front door, and Micah immediately realized what she meant by crowded.

Family was everywhere. Grandparents on the sofa and chairs. More people sitting around a table in the dining room. A little girl on the floor, playing with a truck.

"Hey, everyone," Lorelei called. "I brought a straggler."

"Micah!" Lorelei's mother said, coming forward. "What a surprise." She raised her eyebrows at her daughter. "How did this happen?"

"He was helping serve at the dinner," Lorelei said. "His parents are out of town."

"Welcome," Lorelei's father said, picking himself up off the floor to shake Micah's hand. "It's a little wild around here with the new baby, but we're glad to have you." He turned to Lorelei. "You get all your hours in?"

"I did," she said. "My sheet is signed, and Micah said he'd make sure it got turned in."

"Good, good." Bud turned to survey the room. "I'd pull you up a chair, but we're a little short."

"I'm good," Micah said. "The floor is fine."

He sat down next to the sofa, where Betty was talking to Etta Humphries. He hadn't put together that the school secretary would be part of this family, but now he realized that she was Bud's mother.

"Nice to see you, Micah," Betty said.

When Lorelei sat beside him, the little girl picked

up her truck and hurried over. "Look what Grampa got me," she said, holding it up proudly.

"That's great," Lorelei said. "You going to haul some dirt?"

"Fairy dust," she said. She plunked down in Lorelei's lap.

"This is Shila, my niece," Lorelei said.

"Hello, Shila," Micah said.

"I have a brother," Shila told Micah. "He poops."

"I bet he does," Micah said.

"Do you have a brother?" she asked.

The whole room hushed.

Micah's throat tightened. "I do. His name is Josh."

"Where is he?"

Micah glanced at Lorelei, not sure how to handle this. "In heaven."

"Oh, good," she said. "So he's with Great Grampa Stu."

"Exactly," he said.

Shila stood up. "I'm going to find my fairy dust." She toddled out of the room.

For a moment, no one spoke.

Then Lorelei said, "I hope somebody's cooking in there, because I've made enough dressing and gravy to last five years."

A women Micah didn't know stuck her head out from another room. "Ten minutes to dinner!" she said. "And good for you, Lorelei. It's important to know how to cook for a crowd."

"That's Mandy's mother-in-law," Lorelei said. "It's a lot of people to meet at once, I know."

It was. But as the day moved on, with dinner served and every chair, bucket and TV tray in use to provide a place to eat, Micah couldn't remember a Thanksgiving filled with more noise and laughter.

Baby Thomas made an appearance, and Mandy's happy exhaustion made Micah wonder what his mother was like at this stage, with Micah a toddler and Josh newly born. He should dig out some photo albums and look. He couldn't imagine her in anything but Gucci and diamonds now.

As the festivities wound down, Betty shooed everyone out of the house to let the new family get some rest. Micah stood by his car with Lorelei, wondering what they might be able to say to each other to bridge the gulf between them.

"When are you headed back to Fayetteville?" he asked.

"Sunday," she said.

"Could I see you before you go?"

Lorelei tilted her head. "Is that a good idea?"

He hesitated. She wasn't making this easy. He might as well ask questions. "Why did you have your sister handle my messages after the party?"

Lorelei leaned against the passenger door, wrapping her jacket more closely around her. She wouldn't meet his eye.

"Micah, you have such a future ahead of you. And

people who match you." She gestured toward her sister's house. "I'm ordinary folk. I underachieve. I hang out in a crowded house on Thanksgiving. We don't fly to Milan. We don't have parties where people wear thousand-dollar dresses. I felt so out of place. Your life is just so different from mine."

So this was what she thought of him.

"I can't change your mind on that?"

She pressed her lips tightly together, as if she were struggling with what she had to say. "I'm really glad you came to dinner with us today. And it was so great to see the kind side of you at the church. But long term, I don't think we could fit."

He disagreed, but clearly arguing his point wouldn't help right now.

"Well, thank you for the dinner. It was a good day. Nice to see what a normal family looks like."

Lorelei stepped away from his car. He thought she might say something else, but then she just nodded.

They parted once more. As he drove away from her house, he felt more and more sure that she was wrong. He wasn't what she assumed him to be. Or if he was, he could change. He had seen what he wanted. And it wasn't the picture she'd just drawn for him of fancy dresses and impressive parties.

It was the life he'd just seen.

Now he had to figure out how to make her believe him.

CHAPTER 22

The semester flew by; graduation was applied for. Before Lorelei could blink, December had arrived, along with her commencement day.

Winter graduation held far less pomp and circumstance than the traditional May date, but the college still bustled with seniors in their caps and gowns.

Lorelei walked the stage with the English majors. Many of them had decorated the flat tops of their hats with rhinestones and paint. Lorelei had simply written the words, "What now?" on hers.

Her three grandparents drove up, as well as Mom and Dad. Thomas was still only a month old, so he and Mandy stayed home. George arrived with little Shila, though, and she wore a teensy graduation gown and posed for pictures with her aunt.

Lorelei spent the afternoon after graduation packing her dorm room. She'd barely gotten to know her roommate, who was a sophomore on the dance team and stayed out for rehearsals until all hours.

It had been a lonely semester, truth be told. Most of her friends had graduated last spring, and she'd felt too mature or out of touch to hang out with the students who still had years, or at least another semester, to go until graduation.

She'd been one of the few students actually trying to run a small business while taking small business classes, though, and applied everything she learned toward her bracelets. She left a few for sale on the platforms she'd used before as a loss leader and for discoverability, but also set up her own web site and shopping cart system to maximize her earnings.

She'd be able to cover her student loans for sure, but living on her own with only jewelry was not practical. She was exploring ways to distribute to stores, though, and knew that eventually she'd need help actually making the bracelets, or else she'd have to scale up her designs into gem stones and precious metals where the markup would earn her more per piece.

Her head buzzed with ideas all the time. Maybe if she could substitute teach for a while, she could save money. And possibly even meet some teenagers she could hire for assembly on the weekends.

She felt her head was no longer in the clouds, but

grounded on finding solutions that made sense for her. With a degree, she could also take other types of jobs. Typing, maybe. Or working as a secretary.

It would work out somehow.

Her dad rapped on the frame of the open door. "Last load?"

"Yeah, this one," she said, passing him a box. Her side of the room was stripped and empty. Her missing roommate wasn't even around to say good-bye, having already left for the holiday. "Bye, Melissa," she said to the girl's bed. "Enjoy having a room to yourself."

She followed her dad out and locked the door. "Let me go turn the key in," she told him. "I'll meet you downstairs."

After this, they'd drive back to Applebottom. Tomorrow night, Grandma Betty and Grandmother Etta were hosting a party for her in the private room at Annabelle's Café.

Then she'd have to figure out whatever would be next.

The so-called party room at the back of Annabelle's Café was not particularly grand.

Micah had only been back there once before. It had been a birthday party for some kid in middle school. Most of the time, the room was closed off.

Micah hadn't gone in yet. He had a terrible case of the nerves like nothing he'd ever felt before.

It didn't matter that he stood before judges to argue cases with hundreds of thousands of dollars involved. Or that, in law school, he'd had to do presentations and come up with legal arguments at the spur of the moment, at times when it felt as if his very future in law was on the line.

Nope. Those were nothing compared to this.

He stood outside the back door of the café, too intimidated to even cut through the kitchen. This side of the building faced a field that ended in pine trees. Annabelle's was literally the edge of Applebottom.

He adjusted the portable speaker on a strap over his shoulder and tried to steady his nerves.

The back door opened unexpectedly.

Flo, one of the waitresses, stepped outside and lit up a cigarette. She took a long drag before she noticed him.

She sucked in a breath, then said, "You scared the living daylights out of me, boy." She peered a little closer at him. "Who are you anyway? Unless I died in the middle of the dinner rush, you ain't Elvis."

Micah held out a white-spangled arm. "It's Micah Livingston. I'm just working up the nerve to go inside."

Flo let out a laugh so intense that it caused her to start coughing. She choked for a moment, beating herself on the chest. "Don't make me laugh. It makes me think my doctor's right, and I ought to quit."

"I thought you did quit," he said.

"I tried," she said. "But everybody's gotta die of something."

Micah was in no position to argue with her at the moment.

"You about to head into Lorelei's graduation party in that get-up?"

"If I don't chicken out."

"Huh. The town lawyer. Scared."

"I'm not perfect."

"Well, you need to get in there. They already had dinner, and as soon as they cut the cake, people will start leaving."

"I'm working on it."

Flo laughed, a deep-throated sound that echoed off the building. "I gotta hand it to you," she said. "That's going to make an impression." She poked him in his sparkly-costumed chest.

"That's what I'm hoping."

Flo blew out a long plume of smoke, then put out the cigarette on the brick wall behind her. She tossed the butt into a trash can by the door. "Tell you what," she said. "I'll take you in there. Looks like you need you some gumption, and if there's anything I got a lot of, it's gumption."

Before Micah could argue with her, she linked her

arm through his and hauled him through the back door.

The cooking staff of Annabelle's all stopped what they were doing to watch them pass. Micah took in deep cleansing breaths. He was committed now.

"I'll take you to the side door, so you don't have to go through the main restaurant," Flo said. "You ready?"

He nodded.

They cut down a short hall with a storage room and Annabelle's private office.

Flo paused at the door on the other end. "You ready?"

Micah adjusted the speaker on his shoulder. "Can you take a peek and make sure it's a good moment to walk in there?"

"All right." Flo inched the swinging door open a crack and peeked through. "The dad's talking," she whispered. "Hold on."

Micah could make out Bud's voice. He was giving a speech about Lorelei.

If he'd played his cards better, he would've been in there, invited. But after the Thanksgiving meal, he'd backed off. Lorelei had made the decision for him.

It was actually Betty who had showed up at his office a week ago to let him know that she couldn't invite him to the graduation party without Lorelei saying so, but if he found a way to make an appearance at the café on Saturday night, she'd try to find an excuse to have him come into the private room.

Micah had turned down that offer, although it was good to know that Lorelei's family was on his side. He considered waiting longer. Then about giving up completely. And then one afternoon an Elvis song had come on the car radio, and practically told him exactly what to do.

It would either work, or he was about to make the biggest fool of himself in Applebottom's history.

Flo backed away from the door. The room was clapping. "They're calling Lorelei up to her cake," she said. "This is your moment." She got out of the way.

Micah drew in a deep breath, punched the button on his phone that would wirelessly transmit the music to the speaker he held, and pushed his way through the door.

Lorelei had just arrived at the cake table, when she heard an unexpected sound. Had somebody cranked up the music?

She turned around to see a perfectly costumed Elvis impersonator walk through the back door.

The man was tall, and a little lean for the costume he wore, but his hair was perfectly sleek, and his large sunglasses gave a decent impression of the singer.

She turned to her dad. "You hired an imper-sonator?"

Her dad's mouth was open in surprise.

She was guessing that was a no. It must have been Grandma Betty.

Elvis began walking along the wall, avoiding the collection of tables holding Lorelei's family and friends.

The entire room watched as he approached her. Something in his stride seemed familiar. He couldn't be the same guy they'd seen in Branson. This one was nervous.

Then he lifted the microphone to sing the first line of the song.

And her heart stopped. *Micah?*

Was that really him? She'd never heard him sing. But maybe?

Elvis closed the distance between them and set down the portable speaker he'd been carrying on his shoulder.

As soon as he got close enough, she knew.

Definitely Micah.

His voice was clear and true, bouncing along with the upbeat song. Maybe not like Elvis, but still perfectly good. He came to the chorus, and Lorelei's eyes sparked with emotion when he arrived at the title line: "I Gotta Know."

She held out her hands, and he took them. She

couldn't believe he had done this. What a crazy, risky, spontaneous thing to do.

And for her. Even though she'd ditched him. Quit seeing him. Given up on him.

The lyrics finished, and Micah said, "Happy graduation, Lorelei."

He let go of one of her hands and took off his sunglasses. The half of the room that hadn't already figured it out gasped.

"You came to my party," Lorelei said.

"I thought Elvis would always be welcome," he said.

"He is."

"What about me?"

That was definitely a tough question. She'd been clear to him that their lives were too different. That they didn't fit.

But then, here he was anyway. As Elvis.

There were things *she* had to know. "What happened with Springfield?"

"Turned down," he said. "I needed a family more than a big career. And I feel like I have one in Applebottom."

His voice was still being picked up and projected through his speaker.

Grandma Betty shouted, "We're your family, Micah."

Several other people chipped in with their own affirmations.

He gave them all a grin, then turned back to Lorelei. "What about you?"

She took him in, those soft eyes gazing into hers. His hands, holding on with strength and assurance.

"Okay," she said. "I might be willing to give it another try."

"That's all I ask."

He slid his arm around her, and they faced the room. "I have a feeling that this family of yours is about to call for an encore," he said. "Are you afraid of a duet?"

"Are you crazy?"

"I feel a little crazy right now."

She studied his face a moment, then said, "Only if you turn that microphone off. I think we should get everyone to sing."

He pulled the microphone cord out of the speaker. "Done. What's your choice?"

"I think I have a good one," she said.

"What's that?" he asked.

"It's Now or Never."

CHAPTER 23

When Micah walked into Tea for Two on the first day of spring, there was a bit of a commotion inside.

Both Topher and Danny from Applebottom Blossoms were crowded around the table, along with Arnold from the barbershop, and Betty.

"Is everything okay?" he asked, hurrying to the corner.

Betty looked up, her little white poodle Clementine in her arms.

"Right as rain," Betty said. "You'll want to see this."

He peeked over Betty's shoulder. Sandy, who decorated cakes in the shop when she wasn't traveling around the country making fancy designs for big events, was showing off a new creation.

Arnold turned to Micah, and he was smiling. This was unusual for the old man, who was well known around town for his gruff demeanor, particularly when some upstart young 'un had gone too long without a haircut.

"Looky there," he said. "I'm on a cake."

He was right. Sandy had made a cake of Town Square. A small version of bald-headed Arnold stood by a red and white striped barber pole.

In the center of the square was the gazebo and the grass surrounding it. Little pebble pathways led to the street, including the parking spaces with perfectly formed cars fashioned from frosting.

"That's Alfred Felmont's Model T!" Danny said. "And Gertrude's 1975 Oldsmobile."

"That she still drives," Betty said.

"Well, it runs," Danny said.

Around the square were all the buildings. Betty's tea shop. Topher and Danny's floral shop. The doggy bakery. And Janine's spa.

"See, that's me," Arnold said, pointing.

"You're better looking in frosting," Betty said.

Danny gestured to the corner shop. "Micah, even your law building is here on the corner."

"Sure is," Micah said. What a crazy detailed cake. He'd helped Sandy with a contract or two with some of the companies that wanted her cakes, but he'd never actually seen one up close. Quite a few small people lined the sidewalks. It was remarkable.

"This must have taken hours," Micah said.

"Days. But look at this," Sandy said. "It's the reason I made this cake. It's a practice run."

She pushed a little button attached to a wire that ran under the bottom of the cake.

Two of the cars that were positioned on the road began driving around the square. A tiny version of Betty, with Clementine on a leash, moved forward between the tea shop and the doggy bakery.

"Don't that beat all," Arnold said, taking off his cap and running his hand over his naked scalp.

Betty elbowed Micah. "Go next door and fetch Lorelei."

"I was supposed to take her lunch," Micah said.

"I'll fix her something in a minute," Betty said. "Just go get her."

Micah pushed out of the tea shop and headed next door to the spa. On weekends, Lorelei manned a little space in the front room where she sold her handmade jewelry.

She was still substitute teaching during the week. But she was taking a night class in business, and gradually expanding both her online business and the retail locations where she could distribute her work. She had two girls making bracelets and necklaces for her, and she stuck to the harder pieces, like the rings and earrings.

Micah knew Lorelei loved what she did, because he often caught her humming Elvis songs while she worked. If you had a job where you sang while you worked, probably it was a good one.

Lorelei's head popped up as he entered the room. "Betty too busy to make a sandwich?" she asked, looking pointedly at his empty hands.

"Your grandmother is hoping that you can go next door for a minute. Sandy has made the most extraordinary cake. Is Janine busy?"

"Yeah, she's waxing somebody." Lorelei grimaced. "That's a job I could not do."

Micah grinned. "Well, come on for a second."

The two of them hurried next door to the tea shop. More people had gathered, including Delilah and Maude.

"Where's Gertrude?" Lorelei asked, trying to peer over Maude's shoulder.

"Oh, that woman thinks someone's going to come in and eat all the pie if she doesn't stand guard," Maude said.

Micah stood behind Lorelei as he admired the cake.

"This is super cute," Lorelei said.

More little figures walked along the path. A man in a bowtie headed toward the corner near the pie shop and met a short dark-haired woman.

"Oh, how adorable," Maude said. "That's when Sandy and Andrew came to have a Centennial meeting at my shop."

Sandy nodded. "There are two more sequences."

"Is it on a delay?" Micah asked.

"It's completely timed." Sandy leaned closer to the cake. "I actually got the idea from how the back seats of Doris's minivan slides up on a track. It's almost completely hidden by a little slit in the carpet. I knew if I could put a track underneath a layer of fondant, the frosting would lay back down after the figure passed on the seam.

A box that formed the doggy bakery suddenly moved, the front door sliding open. A figure of a woman with a giant dog emerged.

"That's Ginny!" Delilah said. "With Roscoe!"

"Which one is Carter?" Maude asked.

"I bet it's that one in the middle," Betty said. "He's holding a football."

They watched the little scene play out as Ginny got dragged by the dog across the street and bumped straight into the man with the football.

"I love it," Betty said. "Somebody call Ginny and tell her to get down here."

"There's one more," Sandy said. "Just watch."

A woman figure was headed along the same path Betty had made with her dog, past the tea shop to the law office. She held something in her hand, but Micah couldn't make out what it was.

But she was blond. And Micah had a feeling that one was Lorelei.

The door to the law office opened, and he saw himself come out in volunteer firefighter gear.

Right as his figure made it out onto the sidewalk, a little spark lit up from the blond figure's hand.

"Oh, no!" Lorelei said. "My craziness is forever memorialized on a cake!"

Everyone laughed.

"That was an Applebottom memory for sure," Maude said.

The firefighter figure approached the girl, and as soon as he arrived, the spark went out.

"Look, he saved her!" Maude said. Everyone clapped.

Except, then the spark started up again.

"Oops," Sandy said. "That wasn't supposed to happen."

She mashed the button, but the flickering continued. Sparks fell on the cake, leaving tiny bits of black soot.

"Hey," Sandy said. "Stop it."

More sparks came out. The cake continued to be marred. Micah licked his finger, reached forward, and shut down the spark with a sizzle.

"Thanks," Sandy said, pulling the figure from the track. "I'll get a different one. Maybe this one is faulty."

"See, I cause trouble even on cakes," Lorelei said.

The group dispersed, still talking about the amazing design.

Micah and Lorelei walk hand-in-hand back down the sidewalk. The chilly weather was already getting beaten back by warm afternoons. The grass on the square was starting to show little green buds.

"So, when are your parents supposed to be back?" Lorelei asked.

"Next week," Micah said. "You ready to see them again?"

"Probably by now they've gotten used to the idea that you're dating beneath your station."

Micah lifted her fingers to his lips and brushed a kiss across her knuckles. "I would call it trading up." He held the door open for her.

Inside was still quiet. Micah leaned over the case of her jewelry. "You have some really nice stuff in here."

"Yeah, I need to photograph more of it and get it online," she said. "Gotta pay my rent."

"Linda treating you any better since she got back from her vacation?"

"Nope. I will forever be the girl who set fire to her lawn."

"She must like you. She let you move back in."

"She likes the money. Grandma Betty says she buys three times the Bingo cards now that I'm back."

"Whatever makes her happy."

Lorelei settled on her stool behind the counter. She slid out a tray with the pieces she was working on. "This makes me happy."

Micah was content to watch her work a while, humming a bit of Elvis under her breath.

A woman came out from the back, walking in small tender steps. Lorelei spotted her, and glanced at Micah. They carefully controlled their expressions.

"Should we go to Branson tonight or cook?" Micah asked.

"Hmmm. How about you make that amazing pasta you do."

"You got it."

Janine came out from the back to look at the appointment schedule. "You two lovebirds being good out here?" she asked.

"Always," Lorelei said.

"All right then. Just don't get in a fight and torch my spa." Janine headed down the hall again.

Lorelei rolled her eyes. "I'm never going to live that down."

Micah reached over and tucked a piece of her hair behind her ear. "I don't mind. It's a reminder of when I realized how irresistible you are."

The sun had just set over the lake as Lorelei sat with Micah on the dock at T-bone's RV Park.

A bunch of the teachers, including Lorelei's friend Candace, had gotten together for an end of summer party on T-bone's beach.

As the afternoon wore on, she and Micah had strayed away from the main party. The end of summer didn't mean that much to her. She wasn't in school anymore. Her job wasn't tied to semesters. Even her niece and nephew were too young to go to school. Funny how a cycle that had once dictated the rhythm of her life suddenly no longer had any consequence.

"The sun's going down," she said. "Should we head back?"

Micah clasped one of her hands in both of his and

lifted her fingers to his lips. "Just another minute or two," he said.

They scooted in a little closer, their arms wrapped around each other as the last red-gold rays of sun dissolved into the lake.

"Okay," he said. "Let's go."

The moon guided them as they crunched along the edges where the sand was thinner, and headed into the main part of the beach. It was curiously dark along the water's edge. In fact, much of the RV Park seemed darker than usual, the only real light coming from the convenience store that T-bone kept open from dawn to dusk.

After a moment, though, even that blinked off.

"Is the power out?" Lorelei asked. They could still see well enough by the moon to walk, but it might be difficult making their way back to Micah's car.

Micah gave a noncommittal grunt.

A flame ignited about fifteen yards from them.

Lorelei stopped. "What is that?"

"Let's see," Micah said.

They walked closer, and Lorelei realized that the light illuminated her grandmother Betty's face.

Something was going on.

"What is she doing here?" Lorelei asked Micah.

"I guess we'll find out," he said.

As they got just a few feet from Grandma Betty, another flame lit another face a few yards beyond her.

Fred. The fire chief.

"This is strange," Lorelei said.

When they reached Grandma Betty, she squeezed Lorelei's hand. "You just keep going, child."

"Okay." Lorelei was thoroughly confused.

As they continued along the edge of the beach, more tiny fires began. Each person was holding a small torch.

"Do you know what's going on?" she asked Micah.

He didn't answer, just squeezed her hand.

They passed Mandy and George, holding Shila and Thomas. Then Grandmother Etta and Grandpa Bart. Then Lorelei's friend Bethany, holding her baby with her husband. Then Candace.

"Is this some new Applebottom tradition that started while I was away?" Lorelei asked. She didn't know what to think. She knew everybody here. But then, she knew everyone in Applebottom.

Next was Janine. Then T-bone and Luke. The two of them held extra torches.

"Here you go," T-bone said, passing them theirs. "Mind you, don't burn down my trailer park."

"Thank you," Lorelei said uncertainly.

Micah led her a little farther along the water's edge. She could see four people silhouetted ahead of them.

"Is that mom and dad?" Lorelei asked.

Still, Micah didn't answer.

As they approached, four more flames flared into

life. Now Lorelei clearly saw the faces of her mother, her father, and Micah's parents. They were all barefoot in the sand, her mother's and Alicia's skirts blowing in the breeze.

So this *was* about her. And Micah. Lorelei could guess now what was about to happen. Her heart began to pound.

Her mom stepped forward to give her gentle hug, both of them careful to hold the torches away from each other. "You make me proud," she whispered.

Lorelei eyes welled up. Perhaps she *had* come a long way since last summer, and her disaster that required the fire department to come.

Suddenly she realized what the town had done. They had taken that hard moment when she set the fire, and turned it into something beautiful.

All along the shore, everyone she loved held a torch, their illuminated faces the only light in the dark.

This was family, not judging you in your hard time, but loving you through it. And celebrating when it came to an end.

"Here, love." Her mother reached over and took her torch from her, and Micah's father accepted his.

Then Micah turned to her and dropped to one knee.

A tear slipped down her cheek. This really was it!

Micah cleared his throat. "The best day of my life was when I took off running down Murray Street to put out a smoldering patch of lawn. Who knew that funny little Lorelei had turned into the woman I would come to love with all my heart?"

Lorelei's eyes spilled over.

"We almost called it quits before we even got started," Micah said, his eyes shining up at her. "But I like to think that getting through all that made us stronger in the end."

She nodded, laughing at how silly they'd been, how they'd let small things get in their way.

"So, Lorelei Mary Spencer, will you do me the honor of becoming my wife?"

Something sparkled in the flickering light. Micah held a ring, a silvery band with a circular diamond surrounded by smaller gems.

For a moment, Lorelei's breath was stuck in her throat. But finally, she found her voice. "I will," she said. "I really, truly will."

He stood up and slipped the ring on her finger, then they laughed when they realized it was the wrong hand and moved it to the other. "That isn't my first, nor will it be my last mistake," Micah said.

A great whoop resounded from somewhere up the shore, and the world got brighter as their family and friends closed in with their torches.

T-bone dropped his into a large fire pit buried in the sand, and the others followed, until a great blaze lit their part of the beach.

Lorelei's mother and Micah's father returned

their torches to them, and theirs were the last to fall into the pile. Luke tossed something into the fire and pretty blue sparks rose up from the flames, disappearing in a trail of colored light.

Micah held her close. Someone turned on a radio, and happy music broke the quiet. Some people danced, and others sat back in the sand.

As the two of them made a slow circle around the fire, Micah leaned in close. "I am the happiest man alive," he said.

"Does this mean I'm allowed to burn things again?" she asked.

He let out a strangled laugh. "I'm not so sure about that."

"Do you mean our house won't have a fireplace? Or a gas stove?"

"Maybe we should go with electric. And one of those TV screens with the flames on it."

"Mr. Micah Livingston, do you think I can't handle a little fire?"

He slipped both his hands into her hair, cradling her head. "I think you are all the fire I need."

And he kissed her, surrounded by everyone who mattered, their feet shuffling in the warm sand, the smell of pine trees and lake water and firewood filling the air.

And unlike every summer that came before, this one was pure love.

They figured it out! Whew!

No matter how different two people are, they can make it work. Micah and Lorelei are proof!

Don't miss their wedding, as witnessed by hard-talking, curmudgeonly Gertrude! Fans who receive text or email messages from Abby receive an exclusive bonus epilogue of the wedding for every book!

Sign up on her web site for email or text ABBYT to 77948 (US only) for text!

What did you think about Luke? Tall, dark, and mysterious! The mayor's son gets a match of his own in a heart-warming book with more dogs and cats than you can stand at Savannah's animal rescue in *The Unexpected Shelter*.

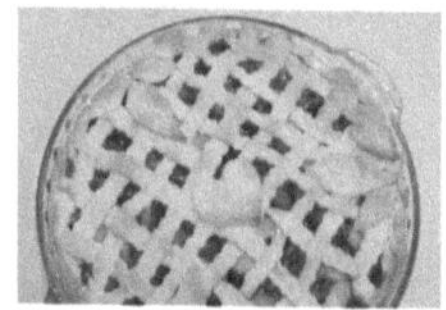

CRUST

• **Your best top and bottom pie crust, unbaked**

(Gertrude, this is book three. Are you going to give up your crust recipe yet?)
(*No.*)
(But, Gertrude, they're going to think you're ungrateful. They've bought book three!)
(*Don't care.*)
(What if they don't have their own crust recipe?)
(*We went over this in book two.*)
(But Gertie, they're your *fans.*)
(*Don't bully me, Maude.*)
(Sorry, readers. I tried.)

FILLING

- **3/4 cup sugar**
(Gertrude, is 3/4 cup enough? Seems like there should be more. Won't the pie be too tart?)
(Only if you want your teeth to rot out of your head.)

- **1 teaspoon cinnamon**

- **1/4 teaspoon salt**

- **1 tablespoon lemon juice**

- **1/4 teaspoon nutmeg**

- **3 pears**
(What kind, Gertie? There's so many!)
(And they're all good. Don't fret about what doesn't matter.)

- **3 large apples**
(I guess I shouldn't fret about what kind here either.)
(Nope. Just know Granny Smith might need a little extra sugar, as they're so tart.)
(Ah-ha!)
(Can it, Maude.)

- **1 egg**

• A bit extra sugar and cinnamon for the top crust, if desired.

INSTRUCTIONS

1. Preheat the oven to 375°F.
2. For the crust: Lay the bottom crust into the pie pan. Place a half-dozen small cuts in the bottom so it will cook evenly.
3. For the filling: Peel and core all the fruit and slice about 1/4 inch thick.
4. Mix the fruit with the sugar, cinnamon, lemon juice, nutmeg, and salt.
5. Spread the filling onto the crust in the pie plate.
6. Layer the top crust over the pie, cutting slits for ventilation. For our pie, we like to do a lattice, but you can top it any old way.

We brush the top of the pie with egg whites and sprinkle a bit more cinnamon and sugar over it before baking.

7. Bake the pie at 375 degrees for 20 minutes, then cover the edges of the pie to avoid burning. Bake an additional 20 minutes. Depending on how you decorated your crust, you may need to bake it slightly longer or shorter to avoid over browning.

Enjoy your pie and don't miss more of Gertrude and Maude in the next Applebottom book: *The Unexpected Shelter* !

ABOUT ABBY TYLER

Abby Tyler loves puppy dogs, pie, and small towns (she grew up in one!) Her Applebottom Matchmaker Society books combine the sweet and wholesome style of romance she loves with the funny, sometimes a-little-too-truthful characters she remembers from growing up in a place where everyone knew everybody's business.

Join her mail or text list for a bonus epilogue for every book, a wedding scene narrated by Gertrude!

The Applebottom Matchmaker Society books include:

- *The Sweetest Match*
- *The Perfect Disaster*
- *The Irresistible Spark*
- *The Unexpected Shelter*
- *The Special Delivery*

with many more planned!